W.

'I'm going to
stand up for

'But Dominic Farq̶   complained. 'He's ̶̶̶̶ going to change.'

Beth found herself wondering about Dominic's image of her—did he ever see her as anything other than an efficient piece of office equipment? 'But I can change,' Beth found herself suggesting.

She thought of her neat, drab clothes which blended into the surroundings, and she thought of Dominic, who would never blend into his surroundings, who would always stand out in the crowd.

The question was, could she do anything about it?

Flora Sinclair was born in and grew up outside London. She went north to study psychology at university, but returned to work in a London hospital. She now lives in Scotland, dividing her time between Glasgow and a remote Hebridean island.

DOCTOR DELICIOUS

BY
FLORA SINCLAIR

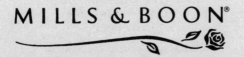

MILLS & BOON®

*First published in Great Britain 1997
Harlequin Mills & Boon Limited,
Eton House, 18-24 Paradise Road, Richmond, Surrey TW9 1SR*

© Flora Sinclair 1997

ISBN 0 263 80442 9

*Set in Times 10 on 11 pt. by
Rowland Phototypesetting Limited
Bury St Edmunds, Suffolk*

03-9711-52794-D

*Printed and bound in Great Britain
by Mackays of Chatham PLC, Chatham*

CHAPTER ONE

'YOU can see he's no well, Doctor.'

Dr Beth Anderson could, indeed, see that the patient was 'no well'. In fact, a superfical glance seemed to indicate that he was very unwell indeed.

'Barry, come and have a seat. I want a word with you.'

Was that a momentary hesitation in his repetitive movements? Beth wasn't sure and if it was it had been so fleeting that it had passed.

'Barry.'

Still no response. The young man continued to stand in the corner of the room, his back to her, as he kicked repeatedly at the skirting-board. He was wearing heavy shoes and the paint had cracked and peeled away from the area he was hitting with unerring accuracy each time. Beth wasn't sure, from where she stood, but she rather thought that the wood had cracked.

Deciding to leave him for the moment, Beth turned her attention back to Mrs Miller. 'Would you like to tell me what has been happening with Barry?'

Mrs Miller was making sideways movements with her eyes and nodding her head frantically in the direction of the hall. Clearly she wanted to get the doctor alone and wasn't too happy about speaking in front of her son. Beth, on the other hand, wasn't too happy about complying with Mrs Miller's wishes. She wasn't sure whether Barry was paying any attention to them or not, but she didn't want to risk fuelling any potential paranoia by talking about him behind his back.

'I'm going to talk to your mother first, Barry. Is that all right?'

The kicking seemed to have quietened slightly and Beth was sure she had done the right thing. Barry might be ill, but he wasn't as out of touch with what was going on as might be thought at first.

Beth sat so that she could keep an eye on Barry, and Mrs Miller sat to the side so that she could also watch her son. It was obvious that she was less than easy with his behaviour. With another quick glance at Barry, she turned her attention back to Beth.

'What is it you want to know, Doctor?'

'Maybe you could start at the beginning and tell me what has been going on. Barry was released from hospital just over six months ago. Is that right?'

She knew that it was but it gave Mrs Miller something to focus on, somewhere to start her story.

'Aye, that's right, Doctor. He'd been in several months by then. On section, like. It's not that he's a bad boy, you know, but when he gets ill it all seems to get a bit too much for him to handle and he gets...well... violent, like.'

'And was he violent when he came out?'

'Och, he was fine. Back to his old self. They'd got him stabilised on that depot medication and he was doing well. Not his real old self, if you know what I mean, but as good as he ever got since he'd been ill.'

'And he was going to the hospital to get his injection?'

'That's right, Doctor. Every two weeks up to the depot clinic. Sometimes I went with him but there was no need really. He got on well with that Sister Michael. Really liked her, he did. She was good with him, too. Firm, like. No messing, but she let him know what was what and he trusted her.'

'So what happened?'

'She went off on maternity leave, didn't she? Upset Barry, that did. He doesn't like change. And he didn't like the new nurse much either. Then he got to thinking

about Sister Michael and her baby. Pleased he was
for her.

'Even went out and bought her a little cuddly toy, but
it got him thinking about how he didn't even have a
girlfriend. Kept on about wanting to get married and have
a family and how no one would want him now. Who'd
want a schizophrenic with no job, no home of his own
and no prospects? he'd say. Well, you can see his point,
can't you, Doctor? Anyway, he seemed to go downhill
after that.'

'In what way?' Beth got her question in quickly, sensing that Mrs Miller might well take all day to get to
the point.

'He stopped going out at all. Not that he was doing
anything much. Just for a wander. Maybe for a couple
of hours when he got his cigarettes. Then he stopped
doing that and spent all his time in front of the telly. Not
that I think he was really watching it.'

'How long did that go on?'

'A couple of weeks, maybe. Anyway, I realised that
he'd missed a clinic appointment, missed his jab.'

Beth's attention was immediately caught by that. 'How
long ago was that?'

'Nearly two months.' Mrs Miller did a quick calcu-
lation. 'Aye, that'd be right.'

'What did you do?'

'Well, I tried to persuade him to go, didn't I? But
when he's in that mood there's no telling him. His father
had a word with him but that just made things worse.
Ended up with a right row.'

'And then?'

'Then I tried phoning the hospital. Spoke to the new
nurse. I don't mind what her name is, but right snooty
she was. Said she wouldn't talk to me but that it was up
to Barry to come for his injection himself.'

'Has he had any medication since then?' Beth could

guess the rest of the story and wanted to get to the heart of the matter.

His mother shook her head sadly. 'No. And it's just got worse. I phoned the clinic again and it was just the same as before so I tried his consultant, Dr Hughes. I could never get to speak to him, but I left a couple of messages with his secretary.'

'Did anyone get back to you?'

Again Mrs Miller shook her head slowly. 'No. I was just thinking I'd have to go up to the hospital and have it out with them when your letter came—so I thought I'd hang on.'

Beth sighed. The letter must have gone out at least ten days ago and it looked as though Barry's condition was worsening rapidly.

'OK. Now, you know why I'm here, don't you?' Beth realised that she had been slightly remiss in explaining—or, rather, not explaining—her position to Mrs Miller and Barry, and hurried to make amends.

'Aye. You're from the Mental Commission. Come to check up on our Barry.'

'That's right. As you know, when Barry was discharged it was under leave of absence. This means he is still technically under a section of the Mental Health Act and can be recalled to hospital if necessary. Barry has been home for six months now and the leave of absence is to be extended. This means someone from the commission has to see him to make sure all is going well.'

That was a slight simplification of the position but Beth thought it would serve.

'Is he going to have to go back into hospital, Doctor?' Mrs Miller's voice shook as she broached the question.

'I'm not sure yet, Mrs Miller, but we'll do whatever is best for Barry.' She looked across at the disturbed young man who was still kicking the skirting board, and wondered how much attention, if any, he had been paying.

'Barry.' She tried to gain his attention. 'Barry, were you listening to what your mother said? Do you agree that was what happened?' Barry didn't respond to her question but it seemed to her that his kicking was getting more violent. 'Barry. Barry, will you come and talk to me?'

Very slowly Beth got to her feet and walked across the room towards him, careful not to make any unduly abrupt movements. She knew from his records that he had been sectioned for overturning a display in a shop when the store dective had approached him because she'd thought he was acting oddly and might need help. She didn't want to trigger something similar if she could possibly help it.

'Barry, will you come and sit down and talk to me?' Beth's voice was calm, soothing, her whole manner aimed at trying to quieten the agitated man. As she approached she noticed that his hands were clenched into fists and his arms were held rigidly by his side. Prudently she took a step back to stay out of reach of those fists, just to be on the safe side. He still gave no indication that he had heard her, and Beth decided to try one last time. 'Barry?'

This time she got a reaction, although not the one she had wanted. Barry turned on her, his face a mask of frustrated fury. 'Bitch,' he snarled, then let forth a volley of abuse which Beth allowed to roll off her with apparent disregard.

Although rationally she knew that he would have responded to anyone in her position in the same way and that it was nothing particularly personal, it was still something she couldn't entirely get used to. A litany of profanities and abusive names always seemed to under- mine her confidence, even if she did not let it show. She wondered if other psychiatrists felt as she did. For a second the image of her boss's features flickered before her eyes. She couldn't imagine anyone or anything undermining his confidence.

'Why don't you get out of here, bitch, and leave me alone?' Barry's tirade was running out of steam and Beth mentally and literally let out her breath. It looked as though he was going to calm down and maybe then she would be able to get something out of him. Her stance relaxed slightly and Barry lunged forward.

Beth didn't have time to do more than gasp but dimly heard Mrs Miller scream in the background. As she waited, almost fatalistically, to feel Barry's hands grab hold of her she realised that it wasn't towards her that Barry had lunged.

It crossed her mind to wonder how much control he had been able to exert to direct his aggression at an inanimate object. With one sweep of his arm he had cleared the small china ornaments and knick-knacks which cluttered the top of his mother's display cabinet. They made a satisfyingly dramatic crash as the broken pieces of china and porcelain went flying, falling to the ground in a random pattern of disorder and chaos which seemed to portray accurately Barry's mental state. For an instant there was stunned silence as all three took in the scene of destruction, and then Barry moved again.

Afterwards Beth went over and over the events in her mind, telling herself that she couldn't have known what he would do and that even if she had, given his superior size and strength, she probably couldn't have stopped him. But that didn't make her feel any better—any less useless, any less guilty. She blamed herself, felt that she should have been able to do something.

With a scream, which sounded more like a child in pain than an adult, Barry flung himself at the cabinet with his arms rigidly outstretched and, as though in slow

motion, Beth watched them connect with the glass panels
in the cabinet doors and then travel through the glass
in a spectacular burst of shards of flying glass and
spurting blood.

Again she heard Mrs Miller scream but this time Beth
was moving, grabbing Barry's arms before he could
inflict more damage on himself by bringing them down
on the shattered glass still held in place in the frame.
Luckily one arm looked as though it had sustained comparatively little damage, although the other had a deep
gash at the wrist which was spurting bright red arterial
blood. Holding the wrist and applying pressure, Beth
looked over her shoulder at an ashen Mrs Miller. The
older woman was nearly as white as her son.

'Ring 999 and get an ambulance here now,' she
instructed, her voice, she noticed, still remarkably even
and controlled.

Mrs Miller rushed from the room and Beth transferred
her gaze back to Barry. His face was a sickly grey and
his eyes were dull with shock but, for the moment at
least, the frustration which had led to violence had been
exorcised.

'How do you feel?' she asked quietly.

'Bloody awful,' came the heartfelt—and rational—
reply.

Beth looked down at the blood dripping onto her beige
skirt and gave a rueful grin. 'I expect you do.'

'What's going to happen now?'

'First we'll get you to Casualty and get this wrist sewn
up. Then we...you're...going to have to come back
into hospital for a bit, aren't you?'

Any thought of contacting Dr Hughes and the community psychiatric nurse to come and see Barry and get
him back on medication was out of the question now.

Mrs Miller came back into the room, the colour just

beginning to return to her face. 'The ambulance is on its way.' She looked totally dazed.

'You'd better get your coat and bag, Mrs Miller,' Beth instructed the shocked woman, 'and a coat for Barry, then you'll be ready when the ambulance comes.'

'Aren't you coming with us?' The anxiety in Mrs Miller's voice rose to border on panic and Beth spoke as soothingly as she knew how.

'Yes, of course I'm coming with you. I'll speak to the duty psychiatrist at Casualty and see that Barry gets settled.'

Dr Dominic Farquhar eased his long frame back in the chair, stretching his legs carefully to miss the waste-paper basket, and massaged the back of his neck. He had been hunched over paperwork for far too long and, for whatever reason, he never felt entirely comfortable working for long at the computer. He stretched both arms and let them drop to his sides. Another half-hour and he would have completed this part of the report and could have a break, before starting on the next lot of data. He would have to collect it from Beth.

At the thought of his junior colleague a slight frown marred his features, drawing beautifully arched brows together and altering his appearance dramatically. He went from being a smoothly good-looking man to someone whose strength of character shone through, whose singled-mindedness was not in doubt. It was rare for him to let his thoughts focus on Beth—there was something about her which was unsettling. He was in no doubt that Dr Beth Anderson was a competent psychiatrist. Nor did he doubt her intellectual ability which, he believed, was in excess of his other colleagues'. She grasped points and arguments quickly, thought clearly and logically and saw to the heart of a problem almost immediately.

It was Beth as a person he didn't understand. Half the

time she looked like a scared rabbit and the rest of the time he forgot she was there. She worked well, he had to give her that, and never complained at all the extra work he sent her way, but still. . .something about her made him uneasy. Whatever it was he wasn't interested enough to try to think it through.

His sister, who had no psychiatric training whatsoever, would have instantly told him what the problem was. She had heard him mention Beth only twice but he had been intrigued. Beth made him feel guilty. And guilt wasn't an experience the great Dr Dominic Farquhar relished.

If he were honest, Dominic would have to admit that he took advantage of Beth—of her intelligence and her willingness to take on extra work. But most of all he was taking advantage of the kind of woman Beth was. Slightly old-fashioned, in that she wouldn't stand up to her boss, she accepted that her role was to do things for other people without complaint.

An unreconstructed male chauvinist pig is how his sister would have—and in the past had—described him, but one who was beginning to feel guilty in that role. What would really have interested and excited her was what would have brought about this change in her brother. The defection of his first wife with a colleague of his seemed to have left barely a mark. The epithets his wife had flung at him, from 'arrogant and domineering' to 'insensitive and workaholic', had hardly caused a ripple in the surface calm of his ambition. The marriage had, in fact, been so brief and apparently lacking in any true communication that she wondered if Dominic even remembered that he had been married.

But since guilt wasn't a common feeling for Dominic he didn't recognise the twinges which assaulted his conscience for what they were. All he thought of was that he wanted the data from Beth now, and not only was the data not waiting for him—neither was Beth.

It was just after five when Beth let herself into the Commission offices in a large, converted house in Glasgow's west end. Getting Barry settled had taken longer than she had anticipated. She would have liked nothing better than to have gone straight home but she didn't want to take case files home with her. Anyway, she wanted to get the incident written up formally before she forgot any of the details.

While she had been waiting with Mrs Miller she had learnt that Barry had cleared the kitchen table with a similar sweep of his arm a couple of days previously and that he had done the same kind of things in the past. His aggression was always directed at things, not people. He had never hurt anyone but himself.

Beth sat at her desk and stared at the computer screen, willing herself to get her report written but just then it seemed beyond her. It was lucky that she hadn't had any more patients to see that day. She'd intended to spend the afternoon working on the figures and tables the Commission's director needed for a presentation on their work but, given the day she had had, he would just have to wait.

She stared down at her blood-stained skirt. It was ruined. She should have gone home to change. Her eyes filled with tears as the trauma of the afternoon caught up with her. She really could do with talking it through with someone. Unfortunately Sally, the other medical officer, and Neil, the social work officer, were both out. The only person in, apart from herself, was the director, Dr Dominic Farquhar.

Beth could just imagine his derision if she went to cry on his shoulder, either figuratively or literally. He would have to know, of course, but when she was a bit more in control. Dominic, forceful and forthright, dynamic and decisive, was more than she could handle on a good day. On a day like today...she didn't even want to think about it.

'Where have you been?' The question shot at her from the door, but Dominic clearly wasn't interested in the answer for, without giving her a chance to respond, he continued, 'Have you got those figures for me yet?' His deep voice grated on her overstrained nerves, causing a shudder to run through her.

'No. I got—'

'What?' He advanced into the room, disbelief giving way to anger. 'Why not?' Again she was given no time to answer. 'You know I need them today. Tonight.'

'I know, but—'

'I thought you were going to work on them this afternoon.'

'I was, but—'

'Since you're here you'd better get on with it now.'

'Can't it wait until tomorrow? I—'

'No, it can't! I want to work on the report tonight and I'm not going to be messed around by your inefficiency.' Without giving her time to utter another word, either in defence or explanation, Dominic turned on his heel and marched out.

Beth knew better than to try to reason with him. Perfectly competent with patients and their families, she dealt less well with her peers and generally badly with her superiors. It was as though all her confidence deserted her. Maybe it was years of her family telling her that she'd never make it as a doctor, of feeling out of place and lacking in social skills all through medical school, but somehow she had ended up passive, unassertive and not a little socially inept.

She was a competent professional woman, at least most of the time. It was only when she had to put herself forward—stand up for herself—that she found herself

lacking the skills. And that lack was never shown up so
clearly as when she was dealing with the domineering
Dr Dominic Farquhar. With him she more often than not
went to pieces.

Sighing, she hit the keyboard.

Two hours later she had most of the work done and had
built up a fine sense of resentment against Dominic.

'Mean, overbearing, arrogant pig. . .'

The computer emitted a pained beep as Beth's errant
fingers hit the wrong key.

'Unfeeling, uncaring, pompous swine.'

She wiped the last command and tried to pay more
attention.

'Selfish, bossy, arrogant bas—'

'You've already used arrogant.'

Beth froze, her little finger again hitting an erroneous
key, making the computer screen go crazy. It couldn't
be. . .yet there was no way she could mistake that voice.
Slowly she swivelled her seat until she was facing the
amused features of her boss. When he didn't say a word
and the silence between them tugged at her taut nerves
she managed to speak, her normally husky voice slightly
squeaky.

'Was there something you wanted, Dr Farquhar?'

The amusement in his face grew. 'Only to find out
who was here. I heard dark mutterings and name-calling
and I couldn't believe it was my quiet Dr Anderson.'

'I'm not *your* Dr Anderson.' Beth blushed as she
spoke, realising that it was only a figure of speech and
one she should have ignored.

'Oh, but you are.' His lazily warm voice caressed the
words and his startling blue eyes were alight with laughter, but the rest of his face was perfectly serious. He
moved from the doorway to come and perch on the edge
of her desk, his long legs in their expensive suiting

stretched before him. 'Now, tell me why you were calling me names.'

Beth stared at him in horror.

'It was me, wasn't it?' he enquired conversationally, and only seemed more amused by her fiery blush. Unable to meet his eyes and lie—or meet his eyes and tell the truth, come to that—Beth kept her head down and her eyes firmly fixed on her hands, clasped in her lap.

A lean, tanned hand, encircled by a pristine white cuff below a dark grey sleeve, came into view and before she'd realised it Dominic had taken her chin in his fingers and was gently forcing her head up until she met his gaze. Beth tried to control her breathing as she was caught in his hypnotic stare.

His dark blue eyes, heavily fringed with thick lashes, seemed unwilling to let hers go, and she was only partially aware of the face which housed them. Dominic's chiselled bone structure, his high cheek-bones, strongly defined jaw and proud, straight nose seemed dwarfed by the power of his eyes. It was the thick, black brows meeting above his nose which gave his face its habitual look of scowling arrogance.

Beth tried to look away, but felt held by his eyes in a way that was strangely new. Dominic's eyes broke away first to rove across the screen, taking in the white lettering on the grey-black background.

'Good. You're working on the detention figures. Are you annoyed with me because I asked you to stay and sort them out?' He sounded very much as though he couldn't care less why she was annoyed with him, or even that she was.

Something gave in Beth. After years of agreeing with everybody—of agreeing with him, of being unfailingly polite and thoughtful—something gave. Maybe, on top of the traumas of the day, she had reached breaking point. Maybe she would have reached it anyway. Instead of the

'not at all' response which hovered on her lips she heard
herself say, 'You didn't ask—you told.'

The amused sparkle in Dominic's eyes hardened fractionally, and he raised one slanting brow at her. 'You
didn't object.'

'You didn't give me much choice.'

'I need the data tonight.'

Beth seethed. She knew it was important but couldn't
help thinking that he could have asked her why she hadn't
got it done. Usually she was highly efficient and kept
strictly to deadlines. Didn't her past record count for
anything?

'Why the panic today, anyway? You normally work
on. Don't tell me you have a heavy date tonight?'
Dominic drawled, and then looked surprised, as though
he had never before considered the possibility of the
quiet Dr Beth Anderson having any kind of date.

It wasn't so surprising, Beth conceded. She was hardly
the material for a rich and varied love life. 'No.' She
didn't even know why she was making such an issue of it.

'Then why the fuss?'

Beth shrugged. 'I'm a bit tired.' Now didn't seem to
be the time to launch into an account of her afternoon.
'We've had a lot on lately and I've had to work late
most nights just to keep up.'

'No more than usual, surely?' Dominic slid from the
edge of the desk to his feet, towering over her.

'These last few months I don't seem to have done
anything but work.'

'You've always coped in the past.' His mouth was
beginning to set in the stubborn line Beth knew so well,
the beautifully shaped lips thinning and tightening—
denying their sensual fullness. 'There isn't room here for
anyone who can't cope. You're a good psychiatrist, Beth,
but you've just got to learn to keep on top of things.'

To Beth this sounded more than a bit patronising, and

she had to bite her tongue to stop the protest which
sprang to her lips from issuing forth. Mutely she nodded,
acutely aware that she didn't dare trust herself to speak.
It might be that the day had been more upsetting than
she had realised for she could think of no other reason
why she might suddenly and astonishingly want to either
scream at her boss or burst into tears. It was a response
which was most unlike her.

Unable to deal with the situation further and wanting
to escape Dominic's penetrating gaze, she turned back
to her computer and the disputed figures. She shifted in
her seat to get into a more comfortable position in relation
to the screen and in so doing caught Dominic's attention. His
glance raked her and then—just as he was turning
away—he swung back, his eyes narrowing.

'What's that on your skirt?' he demanded, leaning over
the desk to get a better view. 'It looks like—' He stopped
abruptly and stared at her.

'Blood,' she finished for him, surprised to see him
flinch at the word.

'Are you—?'

'Don't worry, it's not mine,' she reassured him,
'although I might put the cleaning bill in through
expenses.'

'What happened?' He ignored her attempt at flippancy
and threw the question at her with an urgency which
confused her.

Quickly and concisely she recounted the events of the
afternoon at the Miller house, and was both surprised
and gratified to see the genuine concern in Dominic's
face. Quite why he should have lost colour when she'd
described how Barry had lunged towards the cabinet, she
wasn't sure—until he asked huskily, 'Are you sure he
wasn't going for you?'

'Yes.'

'And you really are all right?'

'Yes. Fine. It wasn't a lot of fun at the time but it's sorted out now.'

'You're sure?'

'I do know how to do my job,' Beth insisted, beginning to feel more than a little aggrieved by the cross-questioning. It was beginning to sound as though he didn't trust her or her judgement.

'I don't doubt that for a minute,' he countered satisfyingly swiftly, putting Beth's fears on that score to rest. 'It's a dangerous position for a woman to be in and—'

'It's a dangerous position for anyone to be in,' Beth admonished immediately, not wanting to give him the opportunity to use this in any way which could be seen as discriminatory.

He shrugged, unwilling to argue the point, but Beth knew that it counted against her—that he felt a man would have prevented the violence from breaking through. When she said nothing else he shrugged again, gesturing down at the screen.

'You might as well pack it in now. It won't hurt me to wait until tomorrow for the figures and you've had a tough day.'

Not willing to concede the point, it was Beth's turn to shrug. 'I told you I'm fine. Now I've started this I might as well finish it.'

'If you say so.' With that he turned and left Beth, fuming, at her computer.

If you wanted him to insist that you should go home and look after yourself you should have known better, she told herself bitterly. The man's a workaholic and expects everybody else to be the same. When has the great Dr Dominic Farquhar seen you as anything other than a dogsbody to do his bidding?

A further hour later she carried the neatly printed copies of the finished data, complete with analysis, into his office, placing them on the desk in front of him when he didn't look up at her entrance.

Beth kept her eyes fixed on the elegant head of hair, its darkness shot through with silver, bent over the papers in front of him. Even at the end of the day it sprang crisply back from his forehead, layers ruthlessly taming the curls so that it looked as unruffled as it had when he'd started out that morning. As though sensing her continued presence, Dominic muttered 'Thank you,' but still didn't look up.

With something suspiciously like tears pricking her eyes, Beth turned and walked across the thick carpeting towards the door. As she reached it she turned automatically. 'Goodnight, Dr Farquhar.'

Whether it was the very slight wobble in her voice, or whether it was the formality of her words, Beth didn't know, but something made Dominic look up sharply.

Hard, assessing eyes raked her from the top of her still-neat head to her flat, highly polished, sensible shoes, taking in all five feet ten of her on the way. What he saw he evidently found wanting, for all he said was, 'Goodnight.'

Beth didn't blame him. There wasn't much to notice. Her dark brown hair swung in a curtain to just above her shoulders, framing her unremarkable features—its natural tendency to wave ruthlessly brushed out. Her pale skin was flawless but didn't, in Beth's opinion, make up for the lack elsewhere.

Her long, rounded body she tried to dress inconspicuously, and nearly always succeeded. Today the beige linen skirt and slightly paler beige blouse merged tidily with the filing cabinets. There was nothing about her to make a man like Dominic Farquhar look at her more than briefly. So used was she to thinking of him as her automaton of a boss that she didn't realise that she had, no matter how fleetingly, just thought of him as a man.

CHAPTER TWO

DESPITE getting home late, Beth was back at work bright and early the next morning at eight o'clock. But still not before Dominic. He was in the same position as she had left him, and only the fact that he had on a different shirt told her that he had been home at all in the interval.

A second glance showed her that although he hadn't been there all night he had probably been working for a good part of it. His normally healthy complexion had an ashen pallor under the tan and there were the beginnings of dark circles under his eyes. Immediately Beth felt the stirrings of sympathy for him. He worked too hard and, because of his size and vigour, it was easy to forget that he was as human as anyone else and that even his formidable energy must flag at times.

How could she begrudge him the help he needed? As she switched the coffee-maker on she remembered their conversation of the night before. It looked as though she wasn't the only one who was working all hours to stay on top of things. Taking her coffee, she entered her room and glanced at her diary. There was a meeting of the full-time commissioners and officers first thing and then she had several local visits to make. With luck she should have time to visit Barry between her scheduled visits and make sure that his admission was progressing smoothly.

How had it happened? Beth had no clear recollection of the discussion but the outcome had been that she was to make a visit with Dominic to carry out a random check on a hospital in the north of Scotland. There had been a couple of worrying rumours and it seemed worth checking out.

She knew that Dominic was aware that she didn't want to go with him. She shrugged. It wasn't for over another six weeks and maybe she could persuade Sally or Neil to swap with her by then. All through the meeting she had been aware of Dominic, scrutinising her. Thank heavens he was off to the States for nearly three weeks. She was beginning to feel like an insect, pinned out for inspection under a magnifying lens, and it wasn't a sensation she enjoyed. She frowned in consternation.

'I wouldn't want to be whoever's caused you to look like that!' Dominic smiled at her, his head tilted slightly to one side in consideration of her bad humour. His approach had been silent and Beth had been caught off guard by him, standing in the doorway to her office.

'No one has done anything,' Beth replied frostily, barely able to glance at him.

His 'Hmm' was wary as he considered her noncommitally. 'It wouldn't be me, then, by any chance?'

She did look at him then, but the speculative expression on his face caused her to look away again quickly. 'Certainly not.'

He looked as though he couldn't have cared less whether he was the cause of her annoyance or not.

'Would you do me a favour while I'm in the States?' Although he phrased it as a request, Beth knew that he didn't really mean it like that. What was coming would be more in the nature of an instruction.

'Could you sort out the leave of absence figures? Most of the data's on the computer but it needs checking. If you could do that and start the analysis we can go over it when I get back.'

'I'm not sure if I've got time,' Beth began hesitantly, chewing on her lower lip while at the same time mentally trying to rearrange her workload to take account of his request. Her mental processes showed clearly on her face as a frown first creased her brow and then gradually cleared. It might be possible if she delayed some of her other work.

'Make time, Beth,' Dominic instructed her. 'You can always make time for something you really want to do.'

Beth sighed. Why was it that she let Dominic walk all over her? Habit, she supposed. But habits could be broken.

On her way out Beth remembered a report she wanted which was in Dominic's office. She hesitated at the doorway but he wasn't there. Knowing that he wouldn't mind her collecting it, Beth went in. She was just leaving when her nose twitched as the scent of Gorgio wafted along the corridor a good ten seconds before the woman wearing it.

'Don't bother to announce me.' Helena Graham swept past Beth without giving her time to react, momentum carrying her through the not-quite-closed door into Dominic's office.

'But he's not. . .' Beth began as a new wave of Gorgio hit her head-on as Helena walked back, giving her time to take in details of the other woman. Tall, but not as tall as Beth, her slenderness made Beth feel that her rounded curves were positively outsize.

Into power-dressing in a big way, Helena Graham was wearing a suit with softly padded shoulders, long jacket and short, straight skirt in a blazing red. With lips and nails to match and blonde hair swept up into a carefully careless knot, she didn't look like the sort of woman to trifle with. And Beth hoped that she had more sense than to trifle with the boss's girlfriend.

'Why didn't you say Dr Farquhar wasn't there?' Helena demanded, and Beth bit back the retort that she'd hardly been given time. Helena had lasted longer than most of Dominic's previous girlfriends and she wondered if at last he was thinking of settling down. She looked again at Helena Graham and wondered why she felt he could do better. The other woman was glamorous, successful and intelligent. What more could Dominic want?

'Well?'

Beth realised with a start that she had no idea what the other woman had just said. It must have shown on her face because Helena spoke again, barely keeping her temper. 'I asked you where Dr Farquhar is. You're not paid to stand there moping.'

'To my certain knowledge, Dr Anderson never mopes.' Neither of the women had heard Dominic come up behind them and he despatched a quick smile to a suddenly embarrassed Beth, before saying to the other woman, 'Hello, Helena. What are you doing here?'

'I thought you could take me to lunch.'

Neither of them took any further notice of Beth as they moved into his office, shutting the door, but she heard him reply, 'I really don't have time for any sort of lunch today.'

Knowing his schedule for the day, Beth couldn't help but agree. She was, therefore, a little surprised to see the two of them emerge less than ten minutes later and hear Dominic inform his secretary, 'I'm taking Ms Graham to lunch. I'll see you in a couple of hours.'

What about your work? she wanted to say, but didn't. What about me? I'm doing extra work for you and you take it for granted and just swan off to lunch. What was the matter with her? she wondered. She had never felt so put upon in the past. Why now?

'What do you think?' Beth smiled encouragingly at the middle-aged woman, sitting opposite her on a shabby but clean sofa.

'I think I could come off the section now, Doctor.' The woman spoke hesitantly, but then said slightly more confidently, 'Aye, I could come off. I'm doing all right now.'

'You certainly seem to be.'

Elspeth Gordon was making up for Barry Miller. She, too, had been on leave of absence from the hospital for six months, but in her case it had been a decision which had worked out well. Stabilised on lithium, she was supported by a community psychiatric nurse and attended a day centre on a regular basis.

For the last four months she had been living in a two-room flat, which she was managing to look after. True, the place was a bit messy but it was basically clean, and Beth had never been one to get as hung up on hygiene and tidiness as some of the other officers. True, poor hygiene and self-neglect could indicate that someone's mental state was deteriorating but she wanted a lot more than that to go on before she thought someone was relapsing.

'The day centre's been a godsend. I couldn't have coped without it.'

'Why's that?'

'Gets me out of the house and meeting people.'

'Do you see anyone, apart from that?'

Elspeth shook her head. 'Not really. I talk to some of the people in the shops, but that's about it.'

'Do you get lonely?'

'What do you think?' Bitterness clouded the older woman's voice, turning it disturbingly harsh, and Beth was momentarily taken aback at the strident sound coming from someone normally so softly spoken. Rallying quickly, she apologised.

'Sorry. That was a stupid thing to say.'

Now it was Mrs Gordon's turn to look surprised. 'I don't remember a doctor ever apologising before.'

'No, we usually think we're right.' Beth smiled gently, not sure how far Mrs Gordon would want to take the conversation, but the other woman seemed to have got herself in hand.

'You usually are. Can't say that I can complain about the treatment I've received over the years. It's not been all sweetness and light, mind, but generally you've all looked after me.'

'And now?'

Elspeth shrugged. 'It's up to me. But it's hard enough anyway for a middle-aged woman to make friends. When you've got a history of mental illness forget it.'

'What about family?'

'My husband left after the first year. Couldn't stand it. Not that I blame him, mind you. I was a handful then, I can tell you. I ran us into so much debt when I was in my manic phase.'

'Shopping?' Beth queried, knowing that it was not uncommon for people in the manic stage of manic-depressive psychosis to go on spending sprees.

The ghost of a smile crossed Elspeth Gordon's face. 'Aye, shopping. I recall ordering a conservatory.'

'You couldn't afford it?' Beth asked, although she was fairly certain that it would have been outside the Gordons' pocket.

'Not only couldn't we afford it, we lived in a third floor flat!' Again Mrs Gordon allowed a half-smile to cross her face. 'It makes a good story now, but at the time it was a disaster. I'd signed some forms so the company was determined to make us pay something. My husband sorted that out, but then it was another thing similar and he was getting fed up.' She stopped and fixed Beth with a steely gaze.

'People always think being manic sounds like fun. Let me tell you, being that out of control was no fun at all. And I still have the debts to prove it!'

'And eventually your husband couldn't cope?'

'Aye. Poor man. I think he never knew what had hit

him. He thought getting married was "settling down"! And there was no one else around to help. There were never many of us in the family. My parents are dead. I've a sister I see about once a year. An aunt somewhere. That's it. My aunt is supposed to be manic-depressive, too, but I've not seen her since I was a kid. Mind you, they call it bipolar depression nowadays, don't they? I don't know whether that sounds better or worse, but it doesn't make much difference to the illness.'

Thinking of her own family and friends, Beth acknowledged how much 'ordinary' people with 'ordinary' lives took for granted.

'It's the weekends when the centre's closed that're the worst. That feels like a week in itself.'

'Maybe there are clubs you can join or—' Beth stopped at the pitying look the other woman gave her. Clearly it wasn't that easy.

'Aye. Maybe.'

She left a little while later, sure that Mrs Gordon was well maintained on lithium and doing as well as she could be expected to—maybe even a little bit better. She was sure that Mrs Gordon's consultant would discharge her and that was the decision she would support.

The memory of Mrs Gordon stayed with her, and she found herself thinking about the woman's friendless state as she drove herself to her own friends that evening. Yes, she had friends now, and a family, but most of her friends were married and she saw less of them than she used to. She didn't want to end up a lonely old woman. She had always assumed that eventually she'd get married and have children. Not that she had been in any hurry, of course, wanting to get her career established first, but somehow. . .somehow it hadn't happened.

Work took up most of her time and there was a dearth of suitable men. It was as though somewhere along the line she had forgotten to get married, and now it looked as if it was too late. Here she was babysitting so that her friends could go out and enjoy their wedding anniversary.

Pulling up outside Cassie's and George's house, she shook her head to free it of her depressing thoughts. What had come over her? Was it just Elspeth Gordon's loneliness getting to her or was there something more? It must be the former, she told herself resolutely. There was nothing wrong with her life.

Nothing that a great man wouldn't improve, a little voice insisted. A great man isn't going to look at me, she answered back. I'm too dull. And, anyway, I don't know any great men. Fortunately Cassie opened the door just as the little voice pointed out that she knew Dominic.

Dominic had been on her mind too much during the last few days. Having come to the conclusion that he was taking advantage of her, she still hadn't worked out how she was going to change things. Standing up for herself was not her forté, and standing up to Dominic was going to be even more difficult.

'He takes advantage of you,' Cassie reproached her. 'You ought to learn to stand up for yourself.'

Beth flinched as her own thoughts were echoed by her friend.

George, Cassie's husband, noticed. 'Do you think we're taking advantage of you, too?' he enquired, an odd expression on his face, as his wife dashed out of the room to complete her make-up.

'Of course not,' Beth said firmly. 'Just try and stop me spending some time with my godson.'

'Just checking,' George laughed easily. 'You just looked. . .'

'It was just that Cassie repeated something I'd been thinking. Take no notice of me.'

Five minutes later, all arrangements having been made, possibilities catered for and the phone number of the restaurant in her hand, Beth was seeing them off.

She spent ten blissful minutes watching Robert George, her seven-month-old godson, sleep before a rumbling stomach sent her kitchenwards in search of sandwiches and coffee. Taking them back to the sitting room, Beth seated herself comfortably with a pile of magazines. Half an hour later she felt as if her life was about to be transformed.

'Sorry, we're later than we thought.'

'Hmm. . .OK.' Beth didn't look up as Cassie came into the room, with George on her heels.

'Beth?'

'Sorry, Cassie. I was miles away. Did you have a good evening?'

'Wonderful. You look as though you've been busy.'

A pile of papers was stacked beside Beth's chair where she had been working, but a magazine was open on the coffee-table.

'Can I borrow this?' She indicated the magazine and Cassie nodded, already on her way to check on Robert.

George, however, picked it up and gazed blankly at it for a moment, before returning it to Beth. 'About time,' was all he said, but gave her an encouraging grin.

About to take offence, Beth realised that there was no point. George was paying her the compliment of being honest with her and also supporting her. With growing confidence, she grinned back.

'What are you two grinning at?' Cassie demanded, giving both her husband and best friend a suspicious look.

'I think the worm just turned,' George said smugly, and drew a reproachful glance from Beth.

'I'd prefer to think of it as a butterfly emerging.'

'So long as you remember there's a chrysalis stage between caterpillar and butterfly.'

'How much have you had to drink?' Cassie demanded

of her husband, looking totally bemused.

'One glass of wine, as well you know,' he answered cheerfully, 'so I could chauffeur you door to door.'

'I suppose you two know what you're talking about,' Cassie complained. 'Maybe one day you'll let me in on the secret.'

Taking pity on her, Beth handed over the magazine. The article was about image and women who had successfully changed the way they looked and behaved and gone on to great success. There were the addresses of several image consultants, including one in Glasgow.

Cassie's eyebrows shot upwards, but all she said was, 'About time', and then wondered why the other two fell about laughing.

Her friends' enthusiasm immediately gave her cold feet.

'Do I really need to do something as drastic as go to an image consultant? Can't I be a bit more assertive and smarten myself up?'

'No!' the other two chorused.

'But I know the principles of assertiveness. All I have to do is put them into practice. I have rights. Other people have rights. I can stand up for my own rights as long as I don't impinge on the rights of others. I don't have to be a doormat.'

'So why hasn't it worked in the past?' Cassie asked, answering herself before Beth had a chance. 'Because you always give in. Because you always feel you have to do the "right" thing, the "nice" thing.'

Beth enjoyed her work at the Mental Health Commission. She had joined with the sense of being on the side of the underdog. The commission existed as an independent body, although funded by the Scottish Office, to oversee psychiatric patients' complaints about their treatment. It also involved following up certain categories of patients, such as Barry Miller and Elspeth Gordon, on extended leave of absence, as well as looking into the type and quality of services provided. If it wasn't quite the high-drama work that she had thought it might be when she'd first gone there it nevertheless had its moments.

She missed the hands-on, day-to-day work of clinical practice, though, and knew that her stay at the Commission would not be for ever. Being what was, to some people, little more than an inspector wasn't going to fulfil her for too long. So why, then, did the thought of leaving the Commission fill her with dread?

For the next couple of days Beth was away from the office, travelling to see patients who lived further afield. She settled back into her routine and forgot about changing her image. She was having no problems com-municating with patients and that was what really mattered. Satisfied that she had cleared up a backlog of leave of absence patients, she returned to the Com-mission, intent on getting the paperwork up to date. Dominic was off to the States in a couple of days and there were still a few things she wanted to check out with him.

He was just coming out of his secretary's office when she passed.

'Beth. Good.' He stopped in mid-stride. 'I want a word about—' He got no further for Irene, his secretary, stuck her head round the door.

'Dr Lyall on the phone for you,' she told him briskly.

'Right.' He looked at Beth. 'I've been trying to get him all day. I'll be along in a minute.' Not waiting for her answer, he headed off towards his office and the waiting call and Beth, with sagging shoulders, made for hers. Why did Dominic persist in treating her as though she was merely there to do his bidding? She was just as much a professional as he was. She was entitled to more respect from him.

Having worked herself up into a state of righteous indignation, when she entered her room and the phone rang she snapped, 'Hello,' into it and was then immediately repentant as Cassie's cheerful voice answered.

'It sounds like a bad moment to call.'

'No, it's OK, really. Things are a bit fraught at the moment.' And that's an understatement, Beth thought to herself.

'I'll be quick, then,' Cassie replied, all brisk efficiency. 'I was only phoning to ask you round tonight. George has to go to a meeting.'

'I'd love to.' To unwind with her friend was just what she needed, Beth decided. Arrangements were quickly made and then a gurgling came on the line, with Cassie's voice in the background. 'Say hello to your Auntie Beth, darling.'

'Hello, Robert, darling,' Beth cooed down the phone, only to almost drop it at the choked sound behind her.

Damn the man. Why did he have to move so quietly? His brows meeting in an angry line, Dominic looked ready to explode. Before he could speak Beth hurriedly said, 'See you tonight,' into the mouthpiece and hung up, looking at Dominic to enquire, 'Did you want something?'

'Some of the time for which you're being paid,' he snarled, and stalked back to his office, the picture of furious male dignity. Hurrying after him, Beth had orders flung at her with a speed which paid no heed to her ability to remember them. Eventually she protested and suggested that they go over them and sort out priorities. Dominic erupted.

'What's the matter? Hoping to have an easier time while I'm away?'

'It's not that,' Beth tried to explain. 'I just don't have time to do everything.'

'You had time to talk to Robert,' he almost yelled at her.

'It was only a couple of minutes.' Explaining about the time seemed more important at the moment than correcting his obviously mistaken impression that Robert was a man and not a baby.

'Hmm.' Dominic's growl told her what he thought of that. 'Sit down, sit down,' he told her impatiently as she hovered by the door. 'I need to fill you in on a new case before I leave.'

He did so rapidly and without dressing anything up. 'A young woman has committed suicide and her family is accusing the staff at the hospital of negligence. They have asked the Commission to investigate. You can make a start while I'm away.'

Beth's heart sank. She had more than enough on her plate as it was, and this would eat into her time dramatically. Other things would have to be put back. 'What about Bob?' she asked, hoping that Dominic would pass the case over to the other medical commissioner.

The anger, which had died in Dominic's eyes, flared back into flashing blue fire. 'What is it with you, Beth, these days? You seem to argue with me at every turn. And you seem to have turned into a clock-watching—' He spluttered to a halt, either unable to think of a suitable description or unwilling to give voice to the one he had.

He was being unfair and Beth suspected that he knew it. Nevertheless, that did not help her deal with the situation.

'Do you like working here, Beth?'

The stark question worried her. What was he suggesting? Mumbling, 'Yes, of course', she turned to leave the room but Dominic stopped her in her tracks.

'As I've said before, you're a good psychiatrist, Beth, but. . .'

Forcing herself to face him, Beth waited for the put-down that was obviously coming. When nothing but silence filled the room she prompted, 'But?' and was rewarded by seeing him momentarily discomposed.

'But you don't seem to know what you want. If you want to get on in this world you've got to learn to stand up for yourself. Can you do that, Beth?'

Impossible to answer, the question hung between them until—unable to either stand the tension or break the silence—Beth stumbled from the room, acutely conscious of his eyes boring into her back. Something had changed in her relationship with Dominic but she didn't know what it was. Or how it had happened.

'So what do I do?' Beth poured out the story to Cassie and George, her bruised feelings soothed by Cassie's interruptions in support of her friend and condemning Dominic out of hand. More than once Beth had wanted to spring to his defence, but something had always stopped her. When she'd finished her story it was George, not Cassie, she turned to for advice, knowing that he would be less partisan and more objective in his comments. Much as she needed Cassie's warm championing of her, right now she needed a more impartial perspective.

'Do you want to leave?' George asked her.

'No. . .' she said cautiously, then added, 'No, I don't,' more certainly. 'But. . .' She stopped and paused, drew in her breath and managed to finish the sentence, 'But I am a total doormat. He walks all over me. And he knows it.'

'So what are you going to do about it?' George wasn't about to let go of the central point until Beth had answered her own question.

'Do what he suggested. Take some control and stand

up for myself,' Beth announced with commendable firmness.

'The man's a chauvinist pig,' Cassie complained. 'He's not going to change.'

'I can try,' Beth suggested, sounding considerably less sure of herself than she had a few moments before.

'Hmm. . .' Cassie sounded less than convinced. 'I know I've only seen him a couple of times, and that briefly, but he *is* a gorgeous brute. I bet he could find any number of willing doormats, if that's what he really wants.'

Beth and George both looked at Cassie in some surprise, and she blushed rosily under their combined gaze. Beth found herself slightly disquieted by her friend's description of Dominic as a 'gorgeous brute'. He was quite good-looking, in a rugged kind of way, and he certainly had magnetism, but. . .

As she conjured up his image it was as though the blinkers which had kept her from seeing him properly fell away, and she realised with a sudden start that what Cassie had said was perfectly true.

The strong jaw and nose stopped him being merely conventionally good-looking, but the high cheek-bones and beautifully curved mouth softened what would otherwise have been harsh. And then there were his spectacular eyes. Those strange navy-blue eyes, which could darken to black and gleam like jet or sparkle like the flames of some other-world fire. Cassie was right. He *was* a gorgeous brute and when he set out to charm he could be devastating. Why had she never really seen Dominic so clearly before?

She turned uncertainly to George, who was grinning unrepentantly at his wife's embarrassment. 'So. . .it all comes out now, does it?' he teased, before turning a more serious face to Beth. 'Cassie may be right, and he may be unwilling to give an inch, but my guess

is that he knows he takes advantage of you. I'm sure
he doesn't want you to leave. You just have to have a
coherent plan worked out for when he gets back.'

It had been George's parting shot before he left the
two women for his meeting that had floored Beth. 'The
trouble is,' he told her, being brutally honest, 'that you
look like a nice lady. Like someone who isn't going to
put up a fight.'

'You mean a doormat.'

'A pretty doormat.'

'But a doormat?'

He nodded. Cassie, ever the honest friend, concurred.
'A total pushover.'

She found herself wondering about Dominic's image
of her—did he ever see her as anything other than an
efficient piece of office equipment? She thought of her
neat, drab clothes which blended into the surroundings,
and she thought of Dominic, who would never blend into
his surroundings, who would always stand out in the
crowd. Unwillingly she found herself remembering
Helena Graham—she and Dominic were two of a kind,
unlike her. The question was, could she do anything
about it?

Carrying home the latest issue of *Vogue* didn't help. An
evening spent looking at anorexic, baby-faced models in
weird and wonderful creations that cost a small fortune
and were clearly never meant to be worn in an office—
let alone seeing patients—convinced Beth that she
needed help.

Without giving herself time to find excuses for not
going through with it, Beth sorted through her papers
and found the magazine she had brought back from
Cassie's. The article she wanted was headed: MORVEN
MCNEIL: IMAGE CONSULTANT. Well, what was the
saying. . .'In for a penny, in for a pound'?

Her heart was in her mouth as she picked up the phone and dialled the after-hours number, almost hoping that there would be no reply. The woman who answered sounded frighteningly self-possessed and the words 'Sorry, wrong number' hovered on Beth's lips. Without warning, Dominic's face swam into view in her mind and she heard him telling her that she had to stand up for herself, his so-blue eyes regarding her with derision. I'll show him, she told herself staunchly, and listened with surprise to herself as she calmly and firmly asked for an appointment as soon as possible.

'You make it sound a matter of life or death,' the other woman half laughed, and Beth was relieved to hear a giggle as she admitted somewhat hesitantly, 'Maybe it is.'

A moment's slience greeted this admission, then she heard, 'This sounds exciting. Come on Saturday.'

As she put the phone down she remembered what she had said to her friends. She was a butterfly emerging. Dominic was off to the States. She had three weeks to be a chrysalis.

CHAPTER THREE

HALF the night Beth lay awake, wondering if she was doing the right thing, while the other half she tossed and turned, telling herself that she had no choice. Her fitful sleep was interrupted by images of Dominic: Dominic pleased at the change; Dominic being appalled; and, what seemed most likely, Dominic not even noticing her new image. In the twilight stage between sleeping and waking Beth found herself remembering the last Christmas party. They had all gone to a dinner-dance at one of the big hotels in the city.

She'd been standing nervously in the doorway, wondering if she could turn and run. The pale grey chiffon dress, which she had been so pleased with when she'd bought it, had looked dowdy and out of place against the bright sparkling colours of the other women. Even as she'd turned to leave a firm hand had grasped her elbow and steered her into the room.

'Over here, Beth,' Dominic's low voice was whispering in her ear, his breath warm against her neck. Involuntarily she shivered and knew that Dominic felt it. As she turned to face him his lips curved into a gently amused smile. Fortunately, before she could say anything she was being introduced to a stunning brunette, poured into a gold lamé dress, who was accompanying Dominic.

'Dance with me, Beth.' Dominic's tall frame was in front of her, his hand held out to take hers, but his words were a command rather than a request.

Not being a good dancer, Beth avoided it whenever she could. 'I'd rather not, if you don't mind,' she muttered, knowing that Dominic couldn't care less, and was then totally bemused when he pulled her to her feet.

'But I do mind,' he whispered in her ear, his voice a low, gravelly growl, as one hand went to her waist.

'I can't really dance,' she protested when she saw Dominic grin.

'Half the people on the floor "can't really dance",' he mimicked. 'All you have to do is sway and shuffle to the music.'

Beth looked around and noticed that most couples were, indeed, dancing as he described, the slow, sensuous music requiring little else from them. Dominic's other hand went to the other side of her waist as he drew her to him.

'Put your hands on my shoulders,' he instructed her, and when Beth gingerly complied she found herself swaying with him in time to the insistent rhythm. Quite when Dominic drew her close she didn't know, only that she was suddenly, horrifyingly, aware that they were much, much closer than they had been, that she was pressed against the long, hard length of his body and that somehow her hands had crept from his shoulders round the back of his neck. With a start Beth jerked away from him and looked up into his face.

Never would she forget the amusement that curved his lips into a smile and fanned out in laughter lines from his sparkling eyes. Beth felt so humiliated that she could have so forgotten herself as to drape herself all over him that she had pulled out of his arms and was walking back to their table before she had quite realised what she was doing.

'Beth, what's the matter?' Dominic's voice was asking urgently under cover of the buzz of conversation.

By then Beth had got herself sufficiently under control to turn a composed face to him and say simply, 'Thank you for the dance, Dominic.'

'Beth—'

The girl in the gold dress insinuated herself between them and Dominic was dragged back to the dance floor before he could finish what he had been going to say.

Beth had done her best to suppress the memory of that night and what she saw as her foolish lapse, but as she remembered it now what came most clearly to mind was Dominic's face and the curious expression that was a mixture of concern and puzzlement. And maybe something she couldn't define.

No matter what changes she had planned for herself personally, the work of the Commission still had to go on. She wrote to the Sullivans, the family of the young woman who had killed herself, and arranged to go and see them as speedily as possible. She read over the notes they had sent in with their complaint. It seemed that Jennifer Sullivan had been hospitalised several times, having both threatened suicide on a number of occasions and made several attempts. She had been hospitalised under section in the past, but this admission had been as a voluntary patient.

Searching out a file on her in the Commission records, Beth was disturbed more by what wasn't in it than what was. There didn't appear to be all the appropriate paperwork appertaining to the death. Closing the file, she pushed it back into place with a thoughtful frown on her face. There was to be a fatal accident inquiry but it had not been heard yet. Would the investigation lead to a verdict the family would be happy with?

'I hear Dominic has offloaded the Sullivan case onto you.' Bob Muir, the other full-time medical commissioner, appeared out of nowhere.

'Yes. Did you want it?' Beth asked the question apparently in all innocence but wasn't at all surprised when the older man threw up his hands in horror.

'Absolutely not. It's all yours.' He laughed as he spoke

but sobered just as quickly. 'I don't envy you dealing with it. There's a lot of bad feeling at St Mungo's at the moment. They've had a run of suicides and everyone is getting very twitchy. Several of the families are up in arms. So is one of the patients' action groups. They're saying there have been too many suicides.'

'And have there?' Beth didn't like the sound of this and wondered what Dominic was doing. At the moment she felt as though she had been thrown to the wolves.

'Doesn't look like it. If you take total deaths by suicide over the last five years they are within the normal limits. They had a long period without any and then a few have clustered together. We all know it goes like that sometimes, although it's not always easy for the public to believe.'

'The Sullivan case was reported in the paper, though.'

'Yes. The family went to the papers themselves. Wanted it blown across the front page, I heard.'

'You seem to have heard a lot.' Beth was becoming suspicious. How come Bob knew all of this?

'Just keeping my ear to the ground, Beth, that's all.' With a conspiratorial wink he was gone, leaving Beth with some very dark thoughts about Dominic and what he had got her into.

Ten minutes into the session Beth knew that she was going to have a fun day. The frighteningly elegant woman who'd greeted her at the door had only to smile to banish any trace of cool reserve and show herself to be warm, friendly, compassionate and, above all, deeply interested in Beth and why she wanted the 'image day' consultation.

'I'll describe what happens over coffee,' Morven told Beth, 'and you can tell me about your life-and-death situation.'

And, very much to her surprise, Beth did.

Totally on Beth's side, Morven narrowed her eyes as

she assessed Beth, muttering almost to herself, 'I think this Dominic is in for one big surprise.' Then, grabbing the coffee-cup out of Beth's startled grasp, she pulled Beth to her feet and said, 'Come on, let's get started.'

She was seated in front of the window, her dark brown hair scraped back and harsh, revealing daylight highlighting every tiny imperfection on her face. Beth looked at herself in the mirror and groaned. Soon, however, as Morven deftly draped coloured silk scarves round her neck and shoulders, she began to appreciate that some colours did more for her than others.

'See how they even out your skin tone and add a translucence to it, as well as making your eyes sparkle,' Morven pointed out enthusiastically. 'Other colours, like this brown, drain you of all colour, making you look like lumpy porridge.'

Beth, faced with the evidence of her own eyes in the mirror, still felt constrained to point out, 'It might be the truth, but you could have put it more tactfully.'

'No time,' Morven explained, whipping a deep raspberry scarf around Beth's neck. 'You're definitely a winter,' Morven told her, having already explained that people were colour-coded by season. 'That means you can wear deep, dramatic colours in cool tones.'

Beth wanted to argue that the colours were *too* dramatic for her, but couldn't dispute what her own eyes were telling her. Rich purples and blues, singing fuschias and raspberry and dramatic black and white all did wonderful things for her. 'You can keep your favourite grey, but we'll enliven it. The safe beiges definitely have to go,' Morven decreed.

'We'll sort out make-up before lunch,' Beth was told, and so it was that she sat down to her salad with Morven, fully made up with a cool beige foundation, a surprisingly pink-in-the-compact blusher swept over her cheeks, her eyes emphasised with grey and a deep, lush crimson on her lips.

Looking at herself in the mirror, Beth could only marvel. 'I didn't know I could look like this.'

'You ain't seen nothing yet, kid,' Morven drawled with a wink as the two fell on their salads with appetites born of hard work.

The afternoon passed in a frenzy of activity as Beth answered questions about her personality and behaviour, and had her figure analysed.

'Romantic with dramatic tendencies', Morven insisted for her clothing personality and added, as Beth continued to look sceptical, 'Truly.'

Beth didn't believe her but as she looked at page after page of pictures she began to change her mind. She recognised outfits that she would love to wear. *If* she had the confidence. And *if* she had anywhere to wear them. As they gazed at a wildly dramatic evening dress of black velvet trimmed with jewels Beth forced herself down to earth. 'It's beautiful. I love it. But I can't wear it to work!'

'Pity,' Morven sighed as she reluctantly turned a page. 'You'd have knocked your Dominic's eyes out, but you're right.' She turned another page. 'This suit you could, though.'

'I'm far too tall,' Beth wailed as Morven insisted that high heels would be great for her, as well as being necessary to complement the shape of the suits they had decided on.

'Nonsense.' Morven wasn't prepared to accept any excuses. 'We're about the same height and *I* wear high heels all the time.'

'That's different,' Beth insisted, only to be left without an answer when the other woman asked why.

Morven looked at her critically again. 'Your posture's good. No slouching—'

'A bully of a PE mistress at school,' Beth reported gloomily.

'You've got good legs and you'll be sensational in high, thin heels.'

'I'll be far too tall,' Beth wailed. 'I'll look conspicuous—'

'You'll look conspicuous in flat shoes,' Morven told her uncompromisingly, 'like a woman who is ashamed of her height.' Not for a moment was she going to tell Beth that by the time she had finished with her she was going to look totally, wonderfully, unmistakably conspicuous.

'Really?' Beth's brow creased in a slight frown, and Morven grinned inwardly. That had worried her!

'How tall is Dominic?' By now Morven felt familiar enough with Beth's boss to refer to him familiarly by name.

'What? Oh, quite tall. . .' Beth sounded distracted, still worrying about her sensible flat shoes. 'About six-three or -four, I think.'

'Perfect.' Morven grinned openly now. 'You can wear heels and not tower over him. He'll still be taller than you, and that will make him feel. . .' she waved expressive hands '. . .at an advantage. Male. . .all those boring macho things.'

'If you're sure. . .?' Beth was wavering, succumbing to a picture of beautiful black suede.

'I am. Positive. Now, when are you going shopping?'

'What?' Beth was startled out of her contemplation of her feet.

'Take a couple of days off and buy some basics. I'll even come with you, if you like.'

'Why?' That wasn't part of the service, Beth knew, and she suspected that Morven was up to something.

'I want to know the end of the story, of course. I want to be involved in the butterfly's emergence and her impact on a boss who deserves every shock he's going to get.'

And, in total accord, the two women grinned.

'It should never have happened.' The anger in the voice of Jenny Sullivan's husband was getting stronger by the minute and Beth was finding it difficult to keep the situation from getting out of hand. 'She was supposed to have been on observation.'

Piecing together the story was a problematic process as Jenny's husband, Bill, and her parents, Esther and Douglas Rankin, were all determined to give their version of the story, and the general series of events was getting lost under a welter of details. Details which might be important at a later stage, but now only served to obscure the main events.

'Let me sum up so far,' Beth interrupted the increasingly heated discussion, 'and make sure I've got things straight. Jenny was ill in hospital with severe depression for several weeks. The drugs she had been given didn't seem to help much and eventually, as a last resort, the consultant suggested they try ECT. Jenny consented to this, although you, Bill, were totally opposed. You think Jenny was brainwashed into having the ECT.'

Even as she spoke, Beth noticed Esther shaking her head a few times. She obviously still believed that her daughter had consented willingly.

'Now, leaving aside the consent for a moment, you all agree that Jenny made some recovery after the short course of ECT. Enough of a recovery, in fact, to be allowed home for the weekend.' She took a deep breath since it was now that the stories began to diverge.

Bill interrupted. 'She went downhill from the moment she came home.'

'No,' Douglas interrupted, 'she was all right when we visited on Saturday afternoon. You're the one who started it. Rowing with her. You should have known better.' He turned to Beth. 'That's what triggered Jenny's decline. She was fine until then.'

'Aye, fine,' his wife agreed.

Beth took up the story. 'You all agree, though, that by Sunday morning Bill was concerned enough to take Jenny back to the hospital.' She stopped and turned to Bill. 'And you insist that you told the nurses that she was suicidal again.'

Looking belligerent, Bill nodded vigorously.

Having decided to listen to the family's story before checking out the hospital notes, Beth was determined to keep an open mind. So far, apart from the minor discrepancy about when Jenny's condition had worsened, the story seemed relatively straightforward.

'Right. And you all agree that Jenny was on observation and that, at some point on Tuesday morning, she had been allowed to go to the toilet unsupervised. The nurse apparently didn't notice for about fifteen minutes that Jenny hadn't returned.' She stopped, wondering how to phrase the next part, but Douglas said it for her.

'Aye, and it took another twenty minutes for them to discover her, hanging from the stairwell, in some God-forsaken part of the building.' His voice trembled, but he went on, 'It was only when we went to visit in the afternoon that we were told of Jenny's. . . Jenny's. . .' His voice broke. 'And no details. Just the bare facts. We phoned Bill to tell him but he wasn't there. Turns out he was already on his way to the hospital. Someone had phoned him with the news.'

Beth left the Sullivans' with Bill's words ringing in her ears. 'It should never have happened.' On the surface it really shouldn't have happened, but Beth knew that with the best will in the world it was sometimes impossible to prevent someone who was completely determined to commit suicide from doing so. Jenny Sullivan had

had a long history of many serious attempts. With a heart-sinking sense of fatalism Beth knew that one day she would have succeeded. If not this time, then another.

The woman had suffered from severe depression and, although she had had periods of time when she was less ill, she hadn't been well for many years. Her drugs had been changed over the years but nothing had seemed to improve things for long. For some time before she died she had been taking lithium. In her case, it hadn't done much good.

Not that that exonerated anyone from negligence. If there had been negligence she would find it, but on the surface it wasn't that clear-cut. She remembered what the family had told her about the way they had found out about the tragedy. Maybe the real problem lay there.

'Where's Dr Anderson?'

Beth was standing facing away from the door and Dominic addressed the back of her head. A head which now had glossy brown hair stylishly layered into her neck and feathering round her ears and the large silver earrings she was wearing. Slowly she turned on her elegant high heels and, inwardly willing her heart to slow down, smiled serenely.

'Good morning, Dominic. Did you have a good trip?'

Whatever she had been expecting, the look of total stupefaction on Dominic's face as a strangled 'Beth?' escaped his frozen lips was everything she could have wished for.

'What the. . .?' he began, before clamping his lips firmly shut on the rest of the sentence. Beth noted with delight the difficulty he seemed to be having with swallowing when he suddenly appeared to get a hold on himself and said with something approaching his normal tone, 'Excellent, thank you, but I have a lot of work to catch up on. Give me a couple of hours, then I'd like an update from you.'

He was halfway down the corridor when Beth's soft, slow, 'Yes, sir!' hit him. Although he didn't stop, say anything, Beth saw his shoulders stiffen slightly. She smiled happily to herself.

She wasn't smiling quite so happily by the end of the afternoon. After his initial shock Dominic had proceeded to behave as though absolutely nothing had changed. Beth could hardly believe it. Admittedly there was an enormous amount of work to catch up on, but to say nothing. . .

All she could do was be thankful that she had had a couple of weeks to get used to her new image herself and for the others in the Commission to get to it as well. If she'd had to put up with the teasing, the admiring glances, some outright envy and the general confusion she had created at the same time as Dominic's total refusal to acknowledge any change it would have been more than she could have borne.

She worked on late, unconscious of time, knowing that now she felt more in control of what she was doing the actual hours of work were less of an issue. She was delighted to see Dominic emerge from his office at six-thirty, looking completely shattered.

'I'm off,' he muttered irritably. 'There's no way I'm going to get caught up tonight.'

'You do look a bit tired,' Beth told him soothingly, and wasn't at all surprised at the sudden glitter of anger in Dominic's otherwise dull eyes and the lowering of his brows. 'Jet lag, I expect,' she carried on in the same controlled, calm voice. 'You need an early night.'

Dominic looked ready to explode, but she couldn't make out what it was that he grunted under his breath as he retreated along the corridor, slamming the door on his way out.

Beth's unhurried walk back to her own office belied her inner state. She felt like a child who had just got the better of her teacher. If she hadn't thought that it would look totally undignified and unprofessional she would have given a little skip of pure joy. Dominic was back and everything was going to work out. Smirking to herself as she entered her office, she acknowledged the truth of what she had so recently learnt. Knowing you looked your best, and that you conveyed a suitable image, really *did* do wonders for your confidence.

Promptly at eleven o'clock Beth stood outside Dominic's closed door, taking deep breaths to slow down her too-rapid pulse. She had made an appointment to discuss her position and workload with him, and now was the moment of truth.

Her hands smoothed down the straight skirt of the pine-green suit she wore and pulled the hem of the peplum jacket more neatly into place. Even without the new shoes with their three-inch heels, the elegant lines of the linen suit with its softly padded shoulders and knee-skimming skirt gave her a longer, sleeker silhouette than she was used to. Without giving herself time to think further, she knocked on the door and walked in.

He was on the phone, which threw her slightly. She was hesitating, not knowing whether to go further into the room or to leave, when Dominic beckoned her in and indicated that she should seat herself in the chair across the desk from him.

As she half listened to the call she realised that it was personal and that he was making a date for the weekend. Trying to block out the sound of his voice, Beth found her temper rising. He was doing this deliberately! He knew about their meeting and this was his way of demonstrating just how far down on his list of priorities she came. Carefully keeping a rein on her anger, Beth waited.

'Goodbye, Marianne.' Dominic's deep voice intruded into Beth's dark thoughts and she focused on him with a slight start. Marianne? What had happened to Helena Graham? She had come to believe that the other woman was a permanent fixture in Dominic's life. And she was sure Ms Graham had thought so, too!

'Now, Beth,' he smiled warmly at her, 'what's this about? What's so important that you have to set up a meeting to talk to me?'

She met his open, candid gaze with a smile of her own. 'Our future together, Dr Farquhar. That's what we have to talk about!'

For a moment Dominic looked thunderstruck as he took in her words, and Beth wasn't at all surprised. She was feeling pretty thunderstruck herself. In all her imaginings of how she was going to handle this she had never prepared herself to say anything quite like that.

His brilliant blue eyes narrowed as he met her paler grey ones, but she didn't look away. To drop her gaze would look submissive, uncertain, and would put her at a disadvantage. A disadvantage on which he would immediately capitalise. That his actions might be unconscious—born of his own confidence, his sense of rightness, his upbringing, which allowed him to believe that women should be submissive—wouldn't stop the effect from being the same as if it were deliberate manipulation.

When she did not lower her eyes a speculative gleam came into Dominic's, but before she had a chance to wonder what it meant—or to react to it—his eyes widened and softened, his tense features relaxed and he leant back in his chair, swivelling it sideways as he stretched his legs and assumed an air of a man at one with the world.

'Our future together, Beth?' he asked, his voice deep and husky. 'What can you be suggesting?'

Beth felt a sudden tightening in her stomach and her breath caught on an indrawn gasp as Dominic's blue eyes swept over her, appraising her. Blood rushed to her face and she knew that her cheeks had turned an unbecoming shade of red as she felt the heat in them.

Against her volition, her eyes dropped before his assessing glance and she wanted nothing so much as to run from the room. It was then that she realised that this was part of his strategy. He was deliberately trying to unnerve her. And he was succeeding!

Taking several deep, calming breaths, Beth willed herself to sit still, meet his by now mocking glance and not flinch. It was now or never. If a butterfly were ever to emerge from the chrysalis she would have to fight her way out. As she sat there, allowing Dominic to stare at her—not challenging him but not looking away—she noticed a gradual change come over him. His eyes lost their amused glint and his mouth its sardonic twist, and a new calculating look took their place, a look which almost bordered on respect.

'Well, Beth,' he said at last, 'what is it you want to say?'

She took a fortifying deep breath. 'I've thought things over and—'

'You've decided to leave.' Dominic's words sliced through hers, a statement of fact—not a question.

Beth faltered and stared at him, totally bereft. He wanted her to go! It had all been for nothing. Silently she waited for him to continue but it seemed that Dominic had nothing else to say. His eyes were dark, bottomless pools, no emotion rippling through their still surface.

But as she watched him she saw the slight throb of muscle as a nerve twitched beside his tightly controlled mouth. He wasn't quite as indifferent as he would have her believe. Maybe, just maybe, he thought that she was going to leave and he had wanted to be the one to say

it. To give himself some control. Taking her courage in
both hands, she quietly contradicted him.

'No. I would like to stay.' She was rewarded by the
very slight easing of the tense body and the almost imperceptible sigh as he released his indrawn breath.

'Good.' The word was grunted, deep in his throat as
though he couldn't trust himself to speak.

'I would like to stay,' Beth repeated, feeling much
more sure of herself now that she really believed that
Dominic wanted her to stay, 'but it depends on a number
of things being sorted out.'

'Go on.' The words and tone were neutral and she
couldn't read anything of Dominic's feelings into them.

'You've been using me too much like an assistant,'
Beth told him, and forestalled any comment by adding,
'I know I didn't say anything and that's my responsibil-
ity. But now I need to take more control over my work.'

'OK.' The instant capitulation stunned Beth. Was it
going to be that easy? Surely not? 'Anything else?'

'Yes. I want to register for an MD and use some of
the work I've done already for you as a basis. It needs
a lot more, of course, but it's a start.'

That really shook him. The utter stillness of his body
and the blankness of his expression told Beth that he
might have expected changes, but not this.

'An MD is a lot of work.'

'Yes.'

'I thought you had been complaining about the amount
of work?'

'I realised that it was because I felt I was being used
as a dogsbody. If I can take some control, have some
choice, then it's quite different.'

'I see.'

Beth wasn't sure that he did, but waited to see if he
would ask anything else.

'Why an MD, Beth? What do you want a higher degree for?'

It was a question she had been expecting—indeed, it was a question she had been asking herself—and she wasn't sure that she had a good answer. It just seemed to be a challenge which she should address. But she had to give Dominic some sort of answer.

'You know my work is important to me,' she finally responded. 'Let's just say maybe I'm more ambitious than either of us realised.' And was satisfied to note that, for once, she was going to have the last word.

CHAPTER FOUR

THE hospital notes and nurses' Kardex were full of detail. Jenny Sullivan had been on fifteen-minute observation as suicide risk, and extensive notes had been kept.

Beth read with interest that her parents had visited everyday, usually in the afternoons, and sometimes again in the evenings, although Bill's visits seemed to have been more erratic. The notes showed that Jenny had improved quite substantially after ECT and she had gone home. Also, that her husband had brought her back to the hopsital, as he had said, on the Sunday.

There was not, however, any note that he had reported her to be suicidal. There then followed a description of what had happened on the day of Jenny's death. She was only on half-hourly supervision so it didn't appear to be a problem that she had been allowed to go off to the toilet on her own. Sighing, Beth closed the file and set out to find the ward sister, who might be able to give her a bit more information.

She met up with Dominic in the hospital canteen for lunch. He had spent the morning talking to the unit manager.

'He's being evasive,' Dominic reported, spearing chips and transferring them to his mouth in an abstracted fashion which told Beth that his mind was elsewhere.

'Has he got anything to be evasive about?' Beth pushed her chips round her plate. The canteen food could have been more appetising.

'I don't know.' The frown drawing Dominic's dark brows together indicated his uncertainty. 'On the surface the only real problem is in the paperwork. I suppose there could be some slapped wrists over that, but—' He shrugged. 'Why do I feel there's something we're not being told?'

'Do you think it has to do with Dr Henderson?'

Again Dominic shrugged. 'We know he's been sloppy with the paperwork. He didn't notify the Commission of the death when he should have done. Negligent, certainly, but nothing that contributed to Jenny's death.'

'Maybe he's generally sloppy. Jenny's parents complained not only about the way they were told about Jenny's death but also about how long it took. Nobody contacted them until they reached the hospital for visiting time. That was nearly five hours.'

Dominic's brows shot up at that. 'I hadn't realised that it had been so long. That seems unreasonable.'

'That's what I thought.'

There was silence while they both contemplated the possible reasons for the lack of contact and the effect this would have on the family. Dominic finished his steak pie and chips and Beth gave up with hers, pushing the plate away. A gesture which caused Dominic's brows to arch once more.

'Not to your taste?' he enquired blandly, and smiled as Beth's nose wrinkled delicately. 'Never mind. Let me take you to dinner tonight.'

Beth, whose mind was on Jenny Sullivan, took several seconds to register the invitation. When she did she was quite sure that she had misheard. Raising wary eyes to meet Dominic's, the laughter in his told her that she hadn't. And, what was more, he was enjoying her discomfiture.

'Cat got your tongue, Beth?' He grinned wickedly while Beth took a deep breath to steady her pounding heart.

'Not at all, Dominic,' she returned, hoping that her

voice sounded steadier than her pulse, 'but I am surprised. Why should we have dinner?'

'Why should we not?' he countered smoothly, leaving Beth with no answer. 'I'll pick you up at seven-thirty.'

Sister Mary Lambert hadn't been able to see Beth before lunch and now, sitting with her in her cramped office, Beth used all her professionalism to force her concentration onto what the nursing sister was saying and not think about Dominic's unexpected invitation. During the course of their conversation it became clear that Jenny had been a well-liked patient.

'She was in and out so we got to know her quite well over the years. Of course, nursing her wasn't necessarily easy when she was suicidal but we always managed to pull her through.'

'But not this time.'

Mary Lambert winced and Beth felt sorry for her. It seemed that the nursing staff had taken this death very hard. Was that just the usual response to such a tragedy? Staff invariably went over what had happened, trying to piece together what had gone wrong and whether there had been anything they could have done to prevent it. Or was there something more in this case?

'What about her family?'

'The Rankins are fine. We all know them well. They're up here all the time when Jenny's in. Was in,' she corrected herself hurriedly. 'They always wanted what was best for her.'

'And her husband?'

A wary look came over Mary Lambert's face. 'I didn't know him so well. He didn't visit so regularly so...' She hesitated. 'He had an aggressive manner about him and was always hectoring the staff. I think it would be fair to say that he wasn't very popular.'

Beth stored the information away, wondering if it

would lead staff to discount what he had to say.

'When he brought her back to the hospital he said he told the nurse on duty that Jenny was suicidal again, but there's no mention of that in her notes.'

Sister Lambert, her dignity as impenetrable an armour as a suit of steel, rose from her chair to stand ramrod-straight in front of Beth. 'If there's nothing in the notes and staff say that nothing was said then Mr Sullivan said nothing.' Her eyes looked straight ahead, almost ignoring Beth—who took the hint.

'Thank you, Sister, for you help. I'll get back to you.' Taking herself off, Beth felt distinctly uneasy. *Something* was going on, but what?

'Dr Anderson.'

Beth was halted by the tentative voice calling her name in an apparently empty corridor. Looking round, she spied a figure beckoning her from a doorway. Crossing to the older woman, she had faint stirrings of recognition.

'Don't I know you?' she asked, taking in the tiny, bird-like woman in front of her whose very frailty made her seem older than she was.

'Aye. Sure you do. I remember you when you were naught but a wee lassie of a registrar,' the tiny woman laughed, 'and here you are an important doctor from the Commission.'

Beth laughed at the description, her slightly serious face shedding several years as amusement gleamed in her eyes and curved her lips. 'You do wonders for my ego, Mrs Bell,' she told the other woman, relieved that she could place her. She was just about to come out with the social nicety of, 'How are you?' When she recollected where they were. Maybe in the circumstances it would not be the most appropriate greeting.

'You're here about that poor lass, Jenny Sullivan, aren't you?' Martha Bell demanded while Beth was still collecting her thoughts.

Slightly taken aback, Beth prevaricated. 'What makes you think that?' she enquired, whilst privately noting that it was almost impossible to hide anything in a hospital.

Martha wisely ignored Beth and continued as if her supposition had been confirmed. 'There's a lot I could tell you about that,' she confided, her voice dropping to little more than a whisper,

The sound of footsteps echoed hollowly down the corridor, and both women turned to see Mary Lambert approaching them.

'You shouldn't be bothering the doctor,' Sister Lambert spoke at Mrs Bell without meeting her eyes, and barely acknowledged Beth's presence.

Martha was not daunted, however, and Beth was impressed by how the elderly patient was able to stand up to the imposing figure of the sister. Drawing herself up to her full four feet ten inches, Martha smiled kindly at Sister Lambert. 'Don't you fret, Sister. Dr Anderson and me, we're old friends.' Her guileless smile appeared so innocent that that was, in itself, almost suspicious. 'I just wanted to make an appointment to see the doctor. I'm entitled, aren't I?'

'Yes, but there are procedures and—'

Beth thought it time to make her presence felt. 'I'm sure I can squeeze Mrs Bell in when I'm here tomorrow,' she told the sister firmly, 'seeing as how we're such "old friends".'

She didn't miss the appreciative chuckle from Martha Bell, nor the frown of annoyance from Mary Lambert.

The buzzer on the entry phone sounded just as she was clipping on heavy silver earrings. Picking up the receiver in the hall, she said hello calmly, while her heart started a sudden, terrifying pounding.

'Dominic.' His disembodied voice sounded almost harsh through the speaker, and Beth had a moment's doubt about the wisdom of dining with him as she depressed the button which would allow him to open the door to the close.

He had two flights of stairs to walk up and it gave her just enough time to take a steadying breath as she checked her appearance before opening the door to him. The slim black jersey dress with its deep boat neckline clung lovingly to her figure and gave her an allure totally missing in her business suits.

Dominic almost did a double take as he stepped over the threshold into Beth's hall. For a moment he even wondered if he had got the wrong flat. Gone for ever, it seemed, was the dull but efficient Dr Anderson he'd known. The woman confronting him now wasn't even the smartly efficient Dr Anderson he had been getting used to all week. This woman didn't look as though she knew the meaning of the word efficient. She looked sleek, sophisticated, sensuous.

'Is something wrong, Dr Farquhar?' The voice was most definitely Beth's her slightly husky tones sounding absolutely right in this present persona, and he wondered why he had never noticed before how sexy she sounded.

'Dominic,' he corrected automatically, realising that he had been staring as he took in the slightly puzzled look on Beth's face. He cleared his throat. 'You have a nice flat,' he muttered, clearly for want of something to say, as far as Beth could tell, for he hadn't even glanced round the hall and that was all he could see.

As he spoke he forced himself to look at his surroundings, and was surprised by what he saw, causing Beth some secret satisfaction as his expression clearly mirrored his thoughts.

'Did you do this yourself?' he asked, and was impressed almost against his will when she nodded.

The five shades of subtle grey highlighted the lines and high ceiling of the spacious Victorian flat and lent

an air of cool elegance he would never have associated
with Beth. Before this evening, that is. A large, pewter-
framed MacIntosh-style mirror caught his eye and he saw
his bemused reflection. This wasn't what he had expected
of his Dr Anderson but it certainly suited the sophisticated woman at his side.

'You've been holding out on me, Beth,' Dominic
remarked, frowning again. Noting the sudden narrowing
of his eyes, Beth wondered what he meant and her feeling
of unease returned. 'We'd better be going,' he added,
and Beth picked up her jacket and bag which she had
laid ready on the small hall table. The notion that this
evening was going to be a big mistake was even more
firmly planted in her mind.

An hour later she had changed her mind. Seated in a
small, cosily intimate Italian restaurant, she felt more
relaxed than she would have believed possible.

'What are you smiling at?' Dominic sounded as though
he genuinely wanted to know, and that set Beth's heart
racing again. She hadn't expected him to be such a
charming companion. That he was caused her no small
concern. It was proving difficult to maintain a suitable
distance from him. She didn't dare call him Dr Farquhar
but wished she could. It would keep him in his place.
Why she should need to keep him in his place she didn't
begin to question.

Shaking her head gently in response to his question,
Beth allowed her smile to deepen. 'Just pleasant thoughts
about how nice it is here,' she offered smoothly, and was
surprised to see Dominic frown yet again.

'That's a very noncommittal answer,' he told her, as
if she didn't know. 'But, then, you've been noncommittal
all evening, haven't you?'

'What do you mean?' Beth set her wine glass down
with a hand that wasn't altogether steady, and knew with
a sinking heart that as the colour rushed up under her

skin she must look the very picture of guilt. It was too late now to wish that she had simply laughed his comment aside. All she could do was hope that Dominic would treat her question as rhetorical and ignore it. In that she was hoping for too much. It seemed that Dominic was all set to tell her exactly what he meant.

'You're being very polite, Beth,' he told her, his voice ominously soft, 'but you're avoiding anything remotely like a personal conversation.' His blue eyes caught and held her lighter ones, and she felt trapped in their depths.

'I wasn't sure if you wanted to discuss the Sullivan case,' she began, only to be cut off by his angry exclamation.

'Damn it, Beth,' he muttered angrily, 'I didn't bring you here to talk about work.'

Why did you bring me here? sprang to her lips, but she was saved from speaking such dangerous words as Dominic proceeded to tell her anyway, without giving her a chance to respond.

'I want to know more about you. We've worked together now for several years and I know as little about you now as I did then.' He stopped and looked at her expectantly, but still Beth said nothing. She wanted to run from the restaurant—run from his probing eyes and searching questions. She eyed the path to the door but knew she couldn't run in her high heels and that Dominic would catch her before she passed the next table.

That Dominic would chase her, she knew with absolute certainty. He wasn't a man to let anyone run out on him—before he wanted it, that was. Rather than make a scene—and that's what would happen, she recognised ruefully—she smiled calmly at Dominic and hoped that her nervousness didn't show. He couldn't *force* her to talk about herself if she didn't want to, could he? Could he? She had the terrible feeling that Dominic could do anything he wanted.

'Does it really matter?' she ventured when she could bear the silence no longer. 'We've always worked well together, haven't we? I don't know anything about you— outside work that is. . .' Apart from Helena Graham and Marianne and all the other names, she added silently. '. . .but that doesn't—'

'Doesn't matter.' Dominic's voice grated harshly over the words as he completed the sentence for her. 'Are you really as cool, as uninvolved, as you sound, Beth?' His eyes slid over her, moving from the creamy skin of her throat and over the swell of her breasts before returning to her flushed face to hold her eyes. 'Not that cool is quite the word to describe you at the moment,' he added, blue fire sparking in the depths of his eyes.

Her breath catching in her throat, Beth looked around wildly for escape. As she did so her eye collided with that of the young Italian waiter. He took it as a signal that they wanted their plates cleared away and moved towards them, smiling, his gaze moving appreciatively over Beth.

'Did you enjoy your mushrooms?' he asked Beth solicitiously, who realised with some shock that she had little memory of the wild mushrooms in a filo pastry basket, which she had eaten without tasting. She smiled back and nodded her enjoyment, not trusting her voice, and noted Dominic's scowl. What had he got to scowl about?

'How long have you lived in your flat?' he enquired, surprising her with his apparent acceptance of her earlier comments. The question could hardly be deemed personal, except on the most superficial level. Recognising that they would be interrupted again shortly with the arrival of their main course, Beth wondered if Dominic was deliberately keeping the topic of conversation neutral until he could be assured of a longer period of privacy

to interrogate her. Well, if he wanted to know about her
flat she would tell him!

What she had intended to be a long, boring account
of the trials and tribulations of the three and a half years
of her flat ownership hadn't quite worked out like that.
Dominic appeared genuinely interested in her account
of the problems with the roof, possibly because—with
hindsight and secure in the knowledge that everything
was now fixed—Beth could make the disaster of her
ceiling falling in into an amusing story. 'So I woke up
to chunks of plaster raining down on me in the middle
of the night.'

'But you could have been hurt, even killed!' He
sounded appalled.

Beth shrugged it off, laughingly acknowledging, 'My
guardian angel was obviously watching over me,' and
was touched that Dominic demanded to know the details,
as though to convince himself that all was now quite safe
and that she had suffered no harm.

'Bob knew a wonderful man who replaced the cornice,' she told him, 'although the work seemed to go on
for ever and cost more than I could really afford.'

'Bob?' Dominic frowned. 'Bob Muir?' He mentioned
the name of the other medical commissioner with surprise
and not a little displeasure.

'Yes,' Beth answered blithely, the wine she had been
drinking relaxing her so that she didn't notice the shift
in Dominic's mood. 'He'd had similar trouble and—'

'He knew about this at the time?'

'Yes, of course. How else—?'

'But I didn't.' Dominic sounded almost grim, and even
in her slightly befuddled state Beth could not miss his
icy tone.

'Well. . .no.' Of course he hadn't known. He knew he
didn't know. He knew she knew he didn't know. She

shook her head, her thoughts tripping over the complications of the logic involved.

'Why is that?' he demanded, his mouth thinning as his eyes raked her face. 'What else does Bob know about you that I don't, I wonder? And just *why* does he know?'

Beth started. What was he talking about? He couldn't be suggesting what his tone sounded as though he was suggesting? Could he? The idea was laughable. Beth shook her head again and vowed to give up wine if this was what it did to her powers of thinking.

She decided to ignore the possible implications of Dominic's convoluted logic and concentrate on her ceiling. That, at least, was a safe subject. She grinned to herself. Maybe neutral would have been a better word. Safe is what the ceiling wasn't—at least at the time.

'I asked for advice,' she patiently explained, 'because I knew he'd had a similar problem.'

'And how did you know that?' Dominic's tone was still icy.

'Everyone knew!' Beth was amazed. For weeks Bob had bored everyone and anyone who would stand still long enough with the problems with the bay window, disintegrating cornice and the unseasonally heavy rain. 'You must have known. . .' Her voice trailed away at Dominic's expression.

'No, I didn't know.' He said the words softly, his face grim and shuttered. 'And I apologise for everything I just said—or implied. I realise now that not only don't I know anything about you but, apparently, I know little about the rest of the people I work with.'

He looked so downcast that Beth almost felt sorry for him. 'That's only to be expected,' she pointed out bracingly. 'After all, you are the director and not—'

'Not interested.'

'I wasn't going to say that. I *was* going to say, not to be disturbed by trivial domestic problems.'

'Hmm.' Dominic didn't sound convinced. 'Maybe it's more a case of people wanting to keep me at a distance. Do *you* want to keep me at a distance, Beth?' Dominic's voice dropped to a husky growl as his hypnotic blue eyes held Beth's grey ones fast in a slightly dazed trance.

Her lips opened to speak but no sound came out, and Dominic watched with fascination as her pink tongue darted out to moisten suddenly dry lips. He leaned forward and caught one of Beth's silently fluttering hands in his. 'Answer me, Beth. Do you want to keep me at a distance?'

For a fleeting instant Beth contemplated telling him that she didn't want him at any distance at all. Then, as though plunging into a pool of icy water, sanity returned. With a supreme effort of will she managed not to pull her hand immediately out of Dominic's warm clasp, but let it lie there passively while she dredged up, from goodness knew where, a serene smile as she forced herself to look at him.

'Of course not, Dominic.' She smiled as she spoke the words, noting the responsive gleam in his eyes before squashing him. 'It's so much easier to work with someone when the two people concerned are able to work in harmony because of their understanding of one another. I think we have always managed that in the past, and hope that we can continue to in the future.'

For a second it seemed to her that Dominic's hold on her hand tightened, but then he let go with a look of distaste, as though finding that what he was holding was something not very pleasant.

Perversely, the moment Dominic let go of her hand Beth would have given anything to have him holding it again. Telling herself not to be so stupid and weak-willed, she put her hands beneath the table so that their trembling was hidden from his all too sharp eyes.

Belatedly she became aware that Dominic was talking

again and sounding more like the old Dominic whom she had known for so many years as her boss, rather than the new, friendlier Dominic she had glimpsed so recently. His expression was one of carefully guarded control, any emotion he was showing that of deliberate policy rather than genuine feeling. Beth had the uneasy sensation that she had thrown something precious away with her prissy, formal speech.

Meanwhile, her rational mind was telling her that this wasn't true, couldn't be true, and that Dominic was only amusing himself when he flirted with her. Why would he be interested in a nobody like her when he had a succession of beautiful, intelligent, successful, high-powered women after him? As the evening progressed Beth understood more and more why women fell for Dominic in droves. Why the quirk of an eyebrow, a lopsided grin, had them flocking to his side. She would need to be careful if she was not to succumb.

The changes she was making to her life had left her very vulnerable. All the old, usual habits—the regular patterns of thought and behaviour—were being swept away, but the new ways of thinking and behaving were not yet part of her—were not second nature. Truly, she was still in the chrysalis stage, despite her outward butterfly appearance. She needed to find new ways to keep Dominic at a distance, to keep him in his proper role— that of her boss.

Firmly pushing the disturbing thoughts to the recesses of her mind, Beth tried to pay attention to what Dominic was saying, and before too long she had forgotten her worries as he charmed and lulled her into a pleasant state of calmness and oneness with him.

It seemed only natural that he should get out of the car with her when they arrived back at her flat, that he should take her key from her nerveless fingers to open the door and let them in and that he should follow her into her hall, closing the door firmly behind them. It was only as he slid her coat from her shoulders that she fully comprehended what had happened, and how subtle Dominic had been. He must have known that she had no intention of inviting him in yet here he was, without a word ever having been spoken.

Some of her fear must have showed in the widening of her eyes because Dominic smiled at her—a friendly, reassuring, everyday sort of smile, with no hint of seduction—and he spoke easily. 'Make us some coffee, will you?' At her nod he murmured, 'There's a good girl.'

Instinctively he knew the layout of her flat and turned away from her, walking unerringly to the living room. By the time Beth rejoined him with the coffee he had lit two lamps, put on some soft music and was lying back in an easy chair, his tie loosened and the top button of his shirt undone. He looked very much at home and Beth, inexplicably, resented it.

'Good girl.' The words, uttered in what Beth considered to be a rather smug tone as she set his coffee down on the low table beside him, annoyed her—for the second time in five minutes.

'I'm not a girl,' she corrected him, her tone cool as she took a seat on the sofa across the corner of the coffee-table from him.

'Oh, but you are.' He smiled lazily at her, his blue eyes appearing black in the dim light as his pupils widened as they ran appraisingly over her. 'You're younger than me.'

'Not by all that much.'

'You look very beautiful tonight.'

'Even if that were true, it has nothing to do with it.'

'Beth, what's the matter with you?' He grinned as though her increasingly bad-tempered tone didn't bother him in the slightest. 'Are you trying to pick a fight? And, if so, why?'

He looked so sure of himself, so in control of the

situation, so much the master that Beth found herself feeling even more annoyed. This was *her* home yet she was the one on edge, the one who stood on uncertain ground. But instead of feeling fearful she felt angry. Not considering that possibly the wine she had drunk was fuelling her heightened emotions, Beth launched into speech.

'I don't like you referring to me as "girl". I'm not.' There was a moment's pause. 'You never used to,' she tacked on.

'Ah, but you've changed, Beth. You're not the person you were. You obviously want to be different and have gone to some lengths to *be* different. You have to expect us poor men who have to live with the transformation to treat you differently.'

'I accept that.' Beth acknowledged his remark seriously, ignoring the teasing voice in which it had been uttered and grinding her teeth in an effort to sound reasonable. 'But I still don't see why you refer to me as "girl".'

'And how would you like me to refer to you?' Dominic asked, sounding surprisingly conciliatory.

'As a woman.' The instant the words left her mouth Beth saw the trap which Dominic had so neatly set for her. A trap, moreover, into which she had blithely stepped.

Silence hung in the air for a moment as Dominic resumed his leisurely appraisal of her face, her body. Under his remorseless scrutiny Beth felt the flush of acute embarrassment colour her face and throat, and felt her fingers curl into her palms until her nails were digging painfully into the soft flesh, leaving vicious half-moon marks in the tender skin.

Heavy with unspoken emotions, the silence lengthened, and with half her mind Beth took in that the music had stopped. As she sat there, unable to move away from Dominic's probing gaze, she felt a strange lethargy steal over her and a fluttering in her stomach. Her legs and arms felt heavy and leaden and she was no longer sure that his visual exploration was unwelcome. It was almost as if it wasn't enough. Her lips parted on a sigh and she felt that time was suspended. Then Dominic broke the spell that was engulfing her.

'But are you a woman, Beth?' he drawled, and instantly she fell back to earth, the impact of his words acting like a slap in the face. He hadn't moved and his gaze held hers while the colour flooded her face more hotly than before.

'I'm not that much younger than you,' she reiterated shortly, unable to say more until she had regained control of her breathing.

'That's not what I meant, Beth, and you know it. It's not even what you meant.' His voice had dropped even lower, throbbing through her confused brain.

Vainly she tried to shake her head—to get some sort of control of the situation—but without warning Dominic was on the sofa beside her. How had he got there? Time and space were playing tricks on her—she hadn't noticed him move. Gently he turned her to face him and she felt totally pliable in his hands—totally malleable to his will. His head came down to hers, blotting out the light from the lamp—blotting out all sense.

'Let's find out how much a woman you are, shall we?' he whispered, his breath a warm breeze grazing her mouth at his lips sought hers.

For that first split second Beth was too stunned to take in what was happening—certainly too shocked to respond—but as Dominic's lips moved over hers, his hands moulding her body to him, an awareness of what was happening flooded through her and almost without volition she wound her arms round his neck and pulled

him to her while she explored his mouth as eagerly as
he was exploring hers.

It had been a long while since she had indulged in
even so much as a flirtation with anybody, and she was
overwhelmed by the sensation Dominic was creating.
She had let herself be pushed back against the sofa
cushions when reality somehow forced itself on her and
she remembered Dominic's other girlfriends. Helena and
the mysterious Marianne.

'No.' She pushed against his chest, frantically trying
to twist her head to get away from that remorseless,
invading mouth. No matter that it was the sweetest sensation she had ever experienced, no matter that her limbs
were trembling and her breasts ached to be caressed by
him, no matter that she wanted his kiss—wanted the
embrace to go on and on. . .

The rational part of her mind recognised all this and
yet was still pushing away from him. As the rational part
of her mind took over from the physical she tried to be
glad that she had rejected him.

Dominic, however, didn't look like a man who felt
that he had been rejected. Reluctantly Beth had to admit
that although he was letting her go slowly he *was* letting
her go. And there was a slow, self-satisfied smile creep-
ing across his handsome features, twisting his lips and
crinkling his eyes. He leaned back against the sofa's
plump cushions.

'I think that answers the question, don't you?' he
drawled, his eyes never leaving Beth's flushed face as his
low, sardonic tone ripped through her fragile defences.

Even knowing that he held all the aces—that she
would never win in a game of words with him—Beth
couldn't bring herself simply to give in. A fighting spirit
she had never known she possessed was pushing itself
to the fore. Summoning all her acting ability, all her
reserves of self-preservation, she willed her eyes to meet

his and forced herself to say quietly, 'And what question was that?'

Blue fire flamed briefly in the depths of Dominic's eyes, and she had the fleeting impression that she had annoyed him as his brows drew together in the most ferocious frown of the evening. But as quickly as the expression had come it was gone, and she was left thinking that she had imagined it.

'That you're maybe not quite a woman,' he spelt out for her. 'Your response was more that of a frightened girl.' His slight irritation had gone, if it had ever existed, and he sounded smugly pleased with himself.

'Maybe my response depends on the man.' As she heard herself lay slight but definite emphasis on the word 'man' Beth was wondering where the words were coming from. Judging from Dominic's thunderous expression, they didn't sound like her. She had succeeded in surprising him as well as angering him.

Irrational pleasure swept through her like a breath of cleansing air. Without knowing quite why, she wanted to anger him. Was it that an angry Dominic was easier to handle than a seductive Dominic?

'Robert makes you respond like a woman, does he?' Dominic ground out between clenched teeth, and ignored Beth's strangled gasp. 'I could make you respond to me, Beth, and you know it.' He was moving towards her again and once more Beth found her hands trapped against his chest as she tried to push him away.

'Even if you could——' she began, trying to placate him. Only to be cut off by Dominic's insistent, 'I could.'

She shrugged and let that comment pass. He was right and she knew she couldn't afford to argue the point with him. He might just take it into his head to prove her right once and for all. 'It's not a good idea to get involved with someone you work with. I know you've always believed that and so do——'

'What's "involved"?' Dominic demanded.

Beth felt her features freeze into immobility, as though they belonged to someone else, as coldness seeped through her, settling like a solid block of ice around her heart. *This* was what she had instinctively been protecting herself against. This casual dismissal by Dominic.

'We could share some good times together, Beth, without it affecting our working relationship.'

Every word sounded like a death knell to Beth and, without knowing how she did it, she forced herself to her feet so that she could look down at him. The lamplight glinted on the grey in his hair, turning it to silver, and Beth knew a moment's weakness—a desire to stretch out her hand and brush through its dark thickness. Resolutely she gripped her hands together in front of her.

'I think you had better go,' she said quietly, and with all the dignity she could muster.

To her surprise, Dominic got to his feet without any argument.

'Running scared?' he asked, and she realised that the smug look was back. 'I'll go now, Beth, but I think we both know I could stay if I really wanted. This isn't the end of the matter between us.'

Hours later, when she could cry no more, Beth tried to analyse why she was so upset. Dominic hadn't behaved in any way that she might not have guessed at. Hadn't she seen him with countless women before now? True, he had never behaved so to her before but, as he had pointed out, she had changed. So, apparently, had he. And, after all, what had he done? He had kissed her. That was all. No big deal. Why was she making such a drama out of it? Tears came again as she pushed the question away. She didn't have an answer for why it should matter. None of it made any sense. Then why was she crying?

CHAPTER FIVE

'WELL, Martha, what have you got to tell me?' Beth wasn't altogether sure she wasn't on a wild goose chase. What could Martha Bell have to tell her that would help in her investigation? The nurses' stories all hung together and there was no obvious negligence. Dominic was off, tracking down Dr Henderson.

'Where to start?' The tiny woman screwed up her face in concentration.

Beth only just managed not to give the traditional answer but waited silently for Martha to begin.

As though sensing that Beth wasn't going to be drawn into game-playing, Martha seemed to give herself a little shake, then plunged into her story. 'The real problem, of course, was the husband. But, then, it always is. Mine—'

'Husband? Jenny Sullivan's husband? Bill?' Beth butted in before Martha could reminisce about her own unhappy marriage.

'Aye. Bill Sullivan. Used to beat her up something terrible, he did.'

'Are you sure?' There was no mention of that in any of Jenny's notes and, although she hadn't liked the man, Beth didn't want to leap to unwarranted conclusions.

'Aye. Sure enough. We used to discuss it. I've known Jenny a few years now. We've met up in here a couple of times. I guessed way back and told her about my Harry. That's how I got her to confess.'

'Why didn't she tell someone? The nurses?' Beth was horrified that the abuse could have been overlooked for so long. 'Surely—'

It was Martha's turn to interrupt. 'You just don't

understand, hen. She thought it was her fault—that she deserved it.'

'But. . .'

'Because he kept telling her so. That she was useless, unattractive. A waste of space. He told her she might as well be dead for all the use she was to him or anyone else.'

'You mean he encouraged her to—'

'Don't say it!' The sudden command, coming from the frail elderly woman, stopped Beth in her tracks and she realised the enormity of what she'd been about to say. She shuddered, the words dying unspoken on her lips. 'Let's just say he wouldn't have done much to stop her.' Martha's faded blue eyes shone surprisingly brightly with anger on behalf of the dead young woman, pinning Beth in their glance.

'If Jenny had been suicidal do you think he would have told the nursing staff?'

Pain dulled the bright, knowing eyes for a moment, then Martha shook her head. 'No. No, I think he would be happy to have her out of the way.'

'Of course you have absolutely no proof of any of this.' Beth and Dominic were in a small office tucked away in a forgotten corner of St Mungo's, surrounded by closed wards which echoed hollowly with every stray sound to come their way.

'No, but—'

'And there's nothing anywhere in the notes to suggest anyone knew.'

'Surely that's negligent. Someone should have tried to find out and—'

'And maybe they did. Maybe they didn't. Maybe Jenny lied. This Martha of yours said she was the only one who knew. Maybe she's the one who's lying.'

'No!' Beth's denial was instantaneous and forceful.

She was sure Martha wasn't lying.

'How can you be so sure? You seem very willing to accept the word of an elderly psychotic woman with nothing to support it. Are you always so willing to believe the worst of men?'

'You haven't met Bill Sullivan. He looks—'

'—"the type"?' Dominic interrupted sarcastically. 'Come on, Beth. You know better than that. There is no type.'

'Jenny's parents didn't like him. Surely that must count for something?'

'My in-laws didn't like me. That doesn't automatically make me a wife-beater.'

The shock hit Beth like a body blow. 'I didn't know you were married.'

'Why should you?' Dominic's attitude was almost one of dismissal, but Beth thought she caught the tightening of his lips before he relaxed in a brief grin. 'And the emphasis is very much on the *was*!'

Much as she wanted to ask him the who, why and where of his marriage, and particularly why his in-laws hadn't liked him, Beth recognised that this was neither the time nor the place. How long had he been divorced? she wondered, then mentally stopped in her tracks. Maybe he wasn't divorced. Maybe he was still married but separated. Or maybe his wife had died.

'So, what have you to go on, other than the fact that you don't like Mr Sullivan?'

'Nothing,' she was forced to admit.

'And that brings me back to what I asked before. Do you usually so readily accept such flimsy evidence?'

She shook her head. 'I know, I know.' She sighed. 'That's not good enough. Nor is it very professional, but without it we don't have anything.'

'Even with it we don't have anything,' Dominic pointed out brutally.

'What? But—'

'Face it, Beth,' Dominic insisted, but his voice had gentled as he forced her to look dispassionately at what they knew. 'Even if he did beat her up he didn't kill her. Even if she was suicidal it's his word against the nurses' as to whether he told them or not. Given what they knew, the treatment Jenny received was perfectly proper. There are signed consent forms for the ECT. Her mother told us Jenny *wasn't* coerced into that. She had had it in the past and knew it helped.'

'So that's it, then?' Beth felt drained and defeated. Rationally she knew that Dominic was right but that didn't make her any happier about it.

'What's making you so worked up about this case?' Dominic asked, almost casually, but Beth heard the undercurrent of genuine enquiry in his voice. 'Why are you so determined to blame someone? You know as well as I do that, while tragic, suicides happen. Some people are going to do it come what may. Jenny was one of those people. You thought so, too, earlier.'

Shrugging, she looked away from him, finding it difficult to answer. It was difficult because she wasn't really sure herself. There was something about Jenny Sullivan's story that spoke to her, made her feel peculiarly close to the dead woman.

Dominic continued, 'This Jenny Sullivan had multiple admissions. If her husband was hitting her regularly don't you think that someone would have noticed something before now?'

Beth sighed. 'Maybe.'

'There's nothing in her record to suggest that she was ever treated for any physical injuries. And what do you have to go on but the word of another patient? What do you know of Martha Bell?'

Reluctantly Beth cast her mind back to her scanty knowledge of Martha, remembering also, as she did so, the older woman's reference to her own abusive husband. Martha had always been paranoid. Had that paranoia led her to extend her experience to believing that the husbands of other patients—even most husbands—were abusive? It seemed more than likely.

'Beth.' Something in his voice made Beth look up and surprise a strangely compassionate look in Dominic's eyes as he gazed at her, a look which—even as she wondered at it—was replaced by his habitual cool, sardonic gaze. A wry smile twisted his lips.

'There is, of course, the matter of the missing paperwork.'

Beth's eyes brightened. 'And the length of time it took to tell Jenny's parents.'

'And husband.'

Beth pulled a face. 'And husband. And the way they were told.'

'We can rap Henderson's knuckles for the paperwork and make him feel very uncomfortable over his general handling of the case in terms of his interaction with the family. He's a perfectly competent psychiatrist but I've heard too many complaints and rumours about the way he treats people to ignore this. It will be a pleasure to give him a scare.' Dominic grinned and Beth, who had been appalled by Dr Henderson's attitude, grinned back and then looked away in confusion as she thought how much younger he looked when he smiled. And her eyes focused on that smiling mouth, and she remembered. . .

'That's all?' Cassie's voice rose an octave in sheer astonishment. 'A couple of kisses? Why are you so worked up?'

'If I knew *that* there wouldn't be a problem, would there?' Beth pointed out with inescapable logic. She had resisted telling Cassie about her dinner date with Dominic, but after a week of Dominic acting as though

it had never happened she only felt more confused and
hoped that a heart-to-heart with her closest friend might
put things into perspective. Maybe she was making too
much of it. Cassie patently thought so.

'On the other hand. . .' Cassie was getting into her
stride now, her brows furrowed together in concentration
as she absent-mindedly conveyed a forkful of cream-
laden pancake to her mouth. '. . .I agree it sounds a bit
out of character.'

'It was Jekyll and Hyde!' Beth's vehemence drew a
sharply curious look from her friend.

'That's a bit strong, isn't it?'

Beth didn't reply, concentrating her attention on the
chocolate crêpe in front of her. Cassie patiently waited
as Beth chewed on a morsel and then repeated, 'Isn't it?'

Putting down her fork with a sigh, Beth forced herself
to meet her friend's open gaze, something she had found
surprisingly difficult since they had begun this conversation. 'I suppose so.' She gave a slight shrug. 'It's just
it was all so unexpected, so. . .' she picked up her fork,
stared at it and put it down again '. . .so. . .'

'Exciting?' suggested Cassie helpfully.

'No!' Beth sounded shocked at the very idea.

'Nice?'

'No.'

'Brief?'

'What?' Beth stared across the café table at the
other woman.

'Did you want him to continue? Is that what this is
all about? You're miffed because he gave up so easily?'

'Don't be silly.' Beth tried to sound scandalised, but
as she felt colour flooding her face she knew that she
didn't look, or sound, as certain about things as she felt
she should. And now Cassie had raised the point she
knew she had to face the possibility that that was part
of the problem.

Dominic had gone back to treating her in his old, indifferent manner—she was once again an efficient, impersonal psychiatrist. Despite their trip to St Mungo's together, he was keeping her at a distance—physically and psychologically. And emotions didn't come into it.

'Let's have another coffee and sort out our shopping lists.' Beth stood up to fetch the coffee, looking around her appreciatively. Prince's Square—with its MacIntosh-inspired metalwork, pale wood, iridescent glass and gilt and glass lifts—was Glasgow's most prestigious shopping centre. Now they were sitting on the top-floor balcony, enjoying a sinful lunch of high-calorie crêpes while watching the young and not so young, the trendy, the glamorous and the ordinary parade by.

As Beth returned the corner of her eye caught a flicker of movement—of familiarity—and she turned to see what, or who, it was. As she did her heart plummeted and the colour rushed to her face, only to drain away as suddenly as it had come.

Dominic was gazing around him, apparently looking for an empty table, with a breathtakingly lovely woman by his side. A family leaving a table caused Dominic to take the woman by the hand and lead her quickly to it. She sank gracefully down into the seat, laughing up at him—apparently giving him instructions about what she wanted to eat as Dominic then went off to the Chinese section. Since she was sitting directly in Beth's line of vision, Beth couldn't help but take in the head of black hair that swung in a riot of casual curls round her heart-shaped face, the stunning figure dressed in sapphire blue, the delicate features and—at least from this distance—the flawless skin.

'What's the matter?'

Beth came out of her stunned trance to realise that Cassie was looking at her with more than a slight trace of concern.

'Nothing. Why?'

'Rubbish. You've gone as white as a sheet. You look as though you've seen a ghost. What's happened?'

'Dominic's here. He's with a woman. And, no, I don't know who she is. And, yes, she's pretty. Very.' Beth answered Cassie's unspoken questions when she could see her friend, although wildly curious, doing her best not to turn round and gawp. 'You'll get to see her when we leave.'

'I'm more interested in having another good look at Dominic,' Cassie told her with devastating honesty. 'I told you I thought the man was stunning and I want to make sure I wasn't mistaken.'

'After what I've just told you, doesn't that make any difference? He was playing with me.' The hurt in Beth's voice was mirrored in her eyes but Cassie didn't seem too perturbed.

'Listen to me, Beth,' she told her friend firmly. 'If I really thought he intended to hurt you I'd want to see him get his come-uppance in no uncertain terms, but I'm not altogether sure that he did.'

'I don't understand.' Sounding like a bewildered child, Beth looked hastily away as Dominic came back into view and tried to focus again on her friend's more comfortable features, only to find Cassie's face disconcertingly serious.

'No, and I don't expect Dominic does either. Look at it from his point of view. He goes off to America, having had a set-to with you—in itself an unusual occurrence. He comes back to find that his efficient but self-effacing Dr Anderson has turned into a glamorous woman who is challenging his authority. He doesn't know how to deal with this new person. He didn't ask for her, didn't expect her, didn't choose her, but he has to learn to live with her whether he likes it or not. It's enough to make you feel sorry for him.'

'Are you trying to tell me I should go back to being as I was before?' Beth sounded even more hurt and bewildered than she had a few moments before, and looked at Cassie as though her friend had betrayed her.

'Don't jump to stupid conclusions,' Cassie replied with something like exasperation. 'I'm only trying to point out that Dominic is probably as confused and unsure as you are.' She prudently ignored the unladylike snort from Beth and continued doggedly, 'He's having to adjust a lot of his ideas about you, Beth, and find new ways of relating to you. That isn't always easy. I know.'

Beth looked up sharply at her friend's tone and Cassie gave her a rueful grin. 'I'm having to adjust, too, you know. You *look* different and that's *making* you different. Even without you trying to be more assertive with Dominic.'

'But I'm the same inside.' Beth's voice rose alarmingly and she looked thoroughly startled by her friend's revelations, and even more so when Cassie shook her head.

'You're not. I'm not saying that you're totally different, but you're bound to change. Already people are treating you differently and you're responding to that. That's good,' she added hastily, seeing the consternation on Beth's face, 'but we *all* have to adjust. You. Your friends. Dominic.

'And my guess is that, partly out of confusion and partly out of tension and not knowing what else to do, Dominic found himself treating you like any other woman he was attracted to. Maybe he meant it, maybe not—who knows? Maybe it was curiosity. He wanted to see how you'd react. Maybe he forgot you worked for him or maybe by then he didn't care. But you rejected him in no uncertain terms. And my guess is that Dominic has been treating you as he has all week as a way of dealing with his battered pride. He's trying to pretend it didn't happen.'

It all sounded very plausible, very reasonable, thought Beth, realising that she hadn't been totally honest with Cassie. She hadn't told her about Dominic's taunts about her inexperience. If he thought she had rejected him because she was frightened he wouldn't be embarrassed, would he?

'Maybe you're right.' Beth sounded very half-hearted in her agreement, causing Cassie to grin at her.

'Of course,' Cassie went on, a mischievous grin in her eyes, 'it doesn't answer the other question.'

'What question?' asked Beth, seeing too late the trap Cassie had laid for her.

'Why, if I'm right, are you so upset about it? Dominic's treating you seriously. He's stopped coming on to you, which you say you don't like, so why are you complaining?'

Why, indeed? Beth couldn't answer that and, since it seemed to be where the conversation had started, she decided that the time had come to move on.

They left the restaurant area without being seen by Dominic, although Cassie had managed to get a good look at him. When Beth would have left the Square altogether Cassie insisted that they stayed.

'I don't often get the opportunity for some self-indulgent window-shopping,' she insisted, 'and I'm not going to be cheated out of it just because you're frightened of Dominic.' It was the right thing to say.

'I'm not frightened,' Beth pointed out with dignity.

And she had no answer when Cassie asked, 'What's the problem, then?'

As they walked into the shop Beth recognised the back of Dominic's head. She would have backed out again but Cassie was already over by one of the display cases, examining the beautiful iridescent glass presented there. Beckoning Beth over, she demanded, 'What about that?'

Looking for a birthday present for her mother-in-law was trying her imagination and she was having great difficulty in making a decision.

Beth moved nearer the dispay which had the effect of also bringing her closer to Dominic than she would have liked.

'It's lovely,' Beth confirmed, 'but won't it be terribly expensive?' She thought she had spoken softly, but as the words left her lips Dominic's head swung round and he stared right at her. How had he heard her above the general noise in the busy shop?

'Beth?' He sounded surprised to see her as his eyes swept over her. Cassie was right next to her and the only person she could possibly be with. As Dominic took this in his whole face lightened with the warmth of his smile. 'Hello.'

'Hello, Dominic.' She would have turned away but he crossed the short distance to them, his smile encompassing Cassie, and somehow Beth found herself introducing her boss to her best friend. As they stood, momentarily lost for the next move, Dominic's companion joined them, the slightly puzzled expression on her face only making her look even prettier. She smiled uncertainly at first, but the smile widened and became more genuinely friendly as Dominic introduced them.

'Marianne, I'd like to you meet Beth Anderson. Beth, this is Marianne, my—'

'You're Beth!' The grin flashed broadly as Marianne looked quickly to Dominic and then back to Beth. 'That explains a lot.'

'Sorry?' Beth looked at the other woman blankly, taking in her dark prettiness.

'I've heard so much about you,' she confided, ignoring the slight frown Dominic was giving her. 'But you're not quite. . .' She tailed off, as though suddenly realising that she was about to put her dainty foot in her mouth.

'Not quite what you expected,' Beth finished for her, pleased to see Dominic look more than slightly embarrassed. What had he been saying about her? She would like to see him squirm. Another thought took over as she wondered *why* they had been talking about her. The idea of Dominic discussing her with his girlfriends didn't appeal at all. Bestowing a frosty glance on Dominic, she explained to Marianne, 'I've had a recent change of image. Maybe—'

'Yes, yes, Dominic said that,' the other girl confessed with totally unselfconscious candour, and Beth was pleased to see colour stain Dominic's cheeks, lying on the high planes of his face. She was glad he felt embarrassed because she certainly did. What she couldn't understand was the warmth with which the other woman was treating her, nor the sense of approval which seemed to emanate from her. Whatever else Dominic had told her it obviously hadn't been the details of last Saturday night. Or maybe he had, and they had laughed together at her.

Trying to block out Dominic from her thoughts as well as her sight, Beth concentrated on the bubbling woman who was now telling them about her new flat. She was younger than Beth had first thought, probably twenty-three or -four. Her fine china-doll features and amazingly bright blue eyes added up to a prettiness which belied what was obviously a very determined personality.

'Do you like this lamp?' Marianne was saying, drawing Cassie into the conversation as well, 'Dominic doesn't approve. What do you think?'

The three women looked at the extravagant lines of the lamp base and the dark, heavy silk of the shade while Dominic stood back, his arms crossed over his chest as he flicked the lamp a disapproving glance before concentrating his attention entirely on Beth.

'It's very. . .' began Cassie, and stopped.

'Dramatic,' finished Beth tactfully.

'But you do like it?' demanded Marianne.

'Yes,' chorused both women definitely.

'It's totally unsuitable,' voiced Dominic. 'It looks as though it belongs in a high-class brothel!'

'Well, you obviously know about that!' Marianne grinned at him, a dimple appearing in her cheek which made her look even younger. 'And as long as it's high-class. . .'

Dominic glared at the offending lamp and growled, 'Do what you like. You always do, anyway. And you're the one who has to live with it.'

Beth immediately took heart from this. It didn't sound as though they had any plans to live together in the near future, whatever else was going on between them.

Marianne flashed him a victorious grin as she turned back to Beth and Cassie. 'Thank you for your support. Dominic can be so stuffy at times. You'll have to come and see it in place.'

The unexpected invitation left Beth momentarily speechless. 'Thank you. That would be nice.' She spoke the conventional words in response to a sharp dig in the ribs from Cassie when the silence went on a moment too long. What was going on? Why was Marianne so determined to be friendly? Most of Dominic's girlfriends usually ignored her. But, then, none had seen her new image. Maybe Cassie was right and it was making more difference than she had anticipated. Maybe Marianne thought that by being friendly to Beth she would get on Dominic's good side.

'I really don't have time today.'

'We have to sort this trip out.' Dominic scowled at Beth as he spoke, looking very fierce around the eyes, but his mouth was more reminiscent of a sulky small boy who couldn't get his own way. And that was the only thing that kept Beth from caving in to his demands.

Angry men were intimidating but sulky boys could be dealt with.

'We have to sort it out today.'

Beth's face took on a faintly resigned air as she looked up at him from her seat behind her desk. He had interrupted her as she was making notes for a meeting that afternoon and her hand, holding her fountain pen, was still poised over the page of notes. She couldn't know that to Dominic her attitude looked like one calculated to indicate that he was a minor annoyance in her busy schedule and that her slight air of exasperation was like a red rag to a bull.

'Whatever you say,' she responded blandly, and was shocked to see very real anger flare in his eyes.

'What's the matter now?' he demanded, his voice heavy with barely suppressed fury. 'You're not too busy to meet with your *boss*, are you?' The emphasis on the word was not lost on her and Beth suppressed another sigh. Dominic was getting more and more impossible.

'Of course not, but I do have a meeting with Bob at three-thirty.'

'You've been seeing a lot of Bob lately, haven't you?' Why did he sound so suspicious? He knew she was involved with Bob in putting together figures for the annual report.

'No more than is necessary,' Beth returned coolly, but some imp of mischief made her add, 'Not that he's not a pleasure to work with. Always so pleasant and cheerful— never moody and unpredictable.' She didn't need to add, 'like some people'. The words hung unspoken in the air between them. A low growl from deep in Dominic's throat told her that she was pushing her luck so she returned to her earlier question.

'I'll see you after that.'

'I shouldn't think we'll be finished before five-thirty.'

'That's fine by me.' Dominic paused, fixing her with an icy stare.

Beth knew when to give in gracefully. She nodded.

By seven-thirty she was tired, fed-up and hungry. Dominic's behaviour could only be described as a go-slow, and Beth was quite sure that it was deliberate. Normally quick and decisive, tonight he was taking the discussion round in circles. As far as Beth was concerned, the last hour and a half had been a complete waste of time. She was wondering how to suggest that they weren't getting anywhere and that they pack up when her stomach gave the message for her with a very undignified rumble.

As Dominic glanced at her she thought she saw a grin tug at the corner of his mouth, but the impression was so fleeting that she decided she had imagined it. But there was a strangely satisfied look in his eyes. Maybe he had just wanted to exert his control over her and prove to them both that he could make her work late when he wanted to. More than once lately his behaviour had bordered on the childish—as though forcing her to his will was all that mattered. A small boy who wanted his own way.

'Sorry about that.' She blushed as she spoke. 'I didn't have time for much lunch.' Another inelegant rumble confirmed the point and this time Dominic did grin.

'Perhaps we had better call it a day before I have you fainting on me from hunger,' he suggested.

Thank heaven for that, Beth thought fervently, as visions of home and supper floated before her tired eyes. I wonder if I can learn to do that to order, she wondered, only to have the wind taken out of her sails when Dominic added, 'We can finish this discussion over dinner.'

'Dinner?' Beth almost wailed the word, her picture of

collapsing in front of the television with a plate of scrambled eggs fading fast.

'You have to eat, don't you?' Dominic was at his most blandly reasonable which, Beth knew to her cost, almost always meant his most stubborn. 'I have to eat. We have to finish sorting this out. . .' He deliberately let the words trail away.

Beth gave in with as good grace as she could muster. 'I'll get my coat.'

As Dominic gave their order to the cheerfully tubby Italian waiter Beth remembered their last meal together and the disastrous outcome. Momentarily overcome by acute embarrassment, she peeped at Dominic through veiled lashes. He looked totally at ease and supremely confident—a far cry from the angry, belligerent man of that morning.

There was no making him out these days. Only a few months ago she would have said that Dominic didn't know the meaning of the word moody. He worked— and played—like a well-oiled machine, and expected the same of others. But now 'fickle' was too stable a word to describe him. Briefly she contemplated whether he was going through a mid-life crisis, albeit a bit early.

'Why did you decide to become a psychiatrist?'

Dominic's question caught Beth off guard. 'I didn't like blood and gore,' she replied without thinking, her standard comment to people who asked but who weren't really interested in her answer. She was amazed to see yellow flecks of anger blaze in Dominic's eyes but he kept his voice even.

'You're determined to keep me at a distance, aren't you, Beth?' If she hadn't known him better she would have thought he sounded almost hurt, but she did know him better. Dominic was invulnerable.

A smile of apology curved her lips. 'Sorry. You caught

me by surprise. I thought you wanted to talk about our visit to Highland.'

'All in good time, Can't we have a civilised conversation as well?'

'If you want.'

A very slight tightening of his lips betrayed the fact that Dominic wasn't happy with her attitude. Beth smiled smugly to herself. He didn't seem to know what he wanted. When she stood up to him he didn't like it, but neither did he seem very happy when she meekly acquiesed. As she watched him his eyes narrowed and she had the uneasy sensation that maybe he knew more of what he wanted than she had suspected.

It only took a couple of seconds' remembrance of their last night out to have her nerves tied in knots. But as the meal progressed Beth relaxed, aided by the potent Italian wine Dominic kept pouring for her and the discreet but persistent flirting of the waiter.

The knowledge that flirting was as natural as breathing to Italian waiters didn't stop her enjoying it. It was a new experience for Beth which went with the new image. It was hard not to respond to him and Beth found herself blossoming under his practised Latin charm in a way that was still new to her. She knew that he didn't really mean it, but was enjoying herself nonetheless.

After a few moments of scowling disapproval Dominic's attitude changed, and he was now smiling benevolently at her unpractised response.

'It's time I was taking you home.'

Instantly Beth started to panic and had to quash it firmly. There couldn't possibly be a repetition of his previous behaviour. He wouldn't want to risk rejection again, would he?

By the time they pulled up outside her flat Beth was more than a little apprehensive. She had hoped that there

would be no parking spaces, which would have made it
easy for her to jump out of the car, but there was one,
right by her entrance, almost as though it were waiting
for them. When Dominic got out of the car with her, her
heart started to pound as though she had just run up the
two flights of stairs to her flat.

'I'll see you to your door,' Dominic informed her,
taking her elbow in a loose, impersonal grip as he ushered
her across the pavement.

Neither spoke as they climbed, their feet echoing hollowly on the stone stairs. Nor was the silence broken as
Dominic took her keys and unlocked her door, standing
back to let her enter. Intending to block his entrance,
Beth swung round as she moved through the door with
one hand out to push it closed, only to find that Dominic
hadn't moved and clearly had no plans to try and gain
entry. Feeling slightly foolish, she took the keys he held
out to her and smiled wanly.

'Goodnight, Dominic. Thank you for dinner.'

'Goodnight, Beth.' His eyes roamed over her face
before they swept down her long, shapely body, moulded
by the pine-green suit. A strange look crossed his face,
a look almost of regret, which Beth wasn't sure she
interpreted correctly, but then the slight smile that tugged
at one corner of his mouth made her apprehensive.

'But you're not Beth any more, are you? Beth was
quiet and uncomplicated, tranquil and no trouble—
you're none of those things. You're exciting and exotic,
very complicated and a lot of trouble. Maybe it would
be easier to remember that if you had a new name to
match your new image.' His eyes slid unsmilingly over
her again and Beth could only stare at him, temporarily
struck dumb. New name? The man was unhinged.

'Elizabeth would suit your more sophisticated moods,
and Liz or Lizzie your more. . .frivolous. . .ones. There's
always Eliza, but I think that sounds too old-fashioned

for the new you. Liza. . .maybe. . . Elizabeth. . . Liza. . .
Yes, they're more you than Beth is.'

Managing to keep her face straight, Beth grinned
inwardly as Dominic made the same mistake that so
many people did over her name. And once more her
name was going to give her the last word. But for the
first time she blessed her mother and whatever strange
impulse had led her to name her daughter.

'That's as maybe,' she answered him coolly, 'but as
my name isn't Elizabeth I wouldn't answer to it.'

'You were christened Beth?' Dominic sounded genuinely surprised, as though the possibility had never
crossed his mind.

'No.'

That shook him even more. 'Then if your name isn't
Elizabeth wh—?'

Beth didn't give him time to finish the question.
'Bethesda,' she said with quiet dignity as she shut the
door in his face, before collapsing into silent giggles at
the look of sheer shock in Dominic's spectacular
blue eyes.

But not before she heard the strangled echo,
'Bethesda!'

CHAPTER SIX

'CAN I come in?'

Bill Sullivan stepped back from the door to let Beth enter, the scowl on his face becoming, if anything, more marked. He didn't ask her to sit down and Beth felt safer standing. Now that she was here she realised how shaky her ground was, and how little right she had to be there.

'What do you want?' He sounded belligerent, but Beth couldn't really fault him for that. It wasn't long since his wife had died and he wasn't being left alone to grieve. A photograph of a pretty, smiling woman on the mantelpiece caught her eye. She turned towards it.

'Aye, that's Jenny just before we got married. When I think how she got when she was ill it's hard to remember how bright and happy she used to be.' He picked up the photograph and ran a thumb over the face, then put it back with hands that trembled. 'When she got so depressed there was no living with her. I used to wonder sometimes if we wouldn't all be better off if she was dead.'

Beth drew an involuntary breath and paled as Bill turned to her.

'Shocked you, have I?' he demanded. 'But, then, you don't know what it's like to watch someone you love change beyond all recognition. It wasn't just me I was thinking of. She seemed to be in so much torment.' He stopped and brushed a hand across his eyes.

'And now?' Beth prompted.

'Now? Now I miss her more than I ever imagined. I tell myself she's at peace—but I'm not. It's my fault.'

Was this what she had come to find out? Now

Beth wasn't sure if she wanted to hear it.

'I should never have married her. Her parents didn't think I was good enough. I'm only a plumber. I make reasonable money, mind, but they wanted her to marry someone in an office. Someone in a *clean* job. Said they'd disown her if she married me. Well, of course, they didn't, but she was always being pulled this way and that between us. It tore her apart. I told her I'd go if that was what she wanted, but it wasn't.'

He sank down in an armchair. 'Poor little Jenny. In the end she couldn't take the strain. As soon as she came home from hospital it started again. They came round here and started running everything down. Wanted her to go back home with them. It seemed best to take her back to the hospital. Much good that did, poor lass.'

Beth put a tentative hand on his shoulder. 'I'm sorry, Mr Sullivan.'

That seemed to bring him back to his usual self. 'Well, what is it you wanted?' he demanded harshly.

'Just to see how you are,' she stammered.

'*I'm* fine,' he said, with heavy emphasis on the pronoun. 'It's a shame you didn't take the same interest in my poor Jenny when she was alive.'

'That's settled, then. We leave after lunch tomorrow and get to the Royal Highland in the early evening.'

'Isn't it all a bit cloak and dagger?' Beth couldn't help feeling that Dominic was over-reacting to a situation they weren't even sure existed.

He frowned at the implied criticism. 'I don't think so. There seems to be a problem with staffing on the night shifts. There aren't enough qualified staff on to be providing proper cover. If even one of the rumours pans out it will have been worth the effort.'

'We'll come back the next day?' Beth had hoped to make the enquiry sound like a statement but knew that

she had failed as she noticed the slight tug at the corner
of Dominic's mouth. He knew that she didn't want to be
away with him for a minute longer than necessary.

'I think we'll stay up an extra day. Plan on being away
two nights, Beth.'

It was Beth's turn to frown, but Dominic mistook the
reason for her unwillingness.

'Robert might not like it but he will just have to lump
it!' He refused to meet Beth's surprised eyes which was,
perhaps, just as well. Her expression gave her away
before she could gain a semblance of control but then
she was left smiling to herself. The thought of Robert so
clearly annoyed Dominic. It did him good to be given a
shake-up every now and then.

'Anything you say. You're the boss,' she told him
with forced casualness. It might be good for him to be
shaken up but it didn't mean that she needed it as well.
She could live without a couple of days in the close
company of Dominic. The journey itself would be enough
of a trial.

Although it had been a number of weeks since the over-
powering perfume had invaded the Commission's
corridors, Beth's brain made the connection at the same
instant that her nose twitched in response and it put all
thought of her current case out of her mind. Gorgio.
Helena Graham was back in Dominic's life—if she had
ever left it. The scarlet-suited blonde swept past Beth
and was halfway towards Dominic's office before the
impact made on her peripheral vision halted her. Swing-
ing round with a suddenness that caused her to stumble
slightly in her ultra-high heels, she raked Beth with an
openly hostile look, demanding, 'Who are you?'

When Beth did not immediately reply Helena was
forced to take a slower, more careful appraisal of the
other woman. Finally the truth sank in.

'Good God!' The blonde was visibly shaken. 'I never dreamed. . . It's incredible. . . How. . .?'

Beth herself was taken aback by the other woman's response. Surely she didn't warrant this sort of exhibition?

But Helena was fast gaining control of her amazement and her pale eyes narrowed to unattractive slits as she focused on Beth. 'When did this happen?' she asked as though she had every right to know, moving as she spoke to inspect Beth from a different angle.

Feeling increasingly uncomfortable, like an insect impaled on a scientist's pin, Beth struggled not to show it and to maintain a polite façade.

'When Dominic was in the States.' Deriving some satisfaction from the annoyance on Helena's face, Beth wondered how much longer she could put up with being treated like some sort of biological specimen.

'Did Dominic put you up to this?' Helena demanded, her high colour clashing unflatteringly with the red of her suit.

'Certainly not!' Beth denied. 'The change was my own idea.'

'Was it now?' The calculating tone in Helena's voice warned Beth to be on her guard. 'I wonder why?'

Beth stood motionless in the face of such unwarranted hostility. Just as she was wondering what on earth she was going to do the mood was broken by Dominic running up the stairs, his shirt-sleeves rolled up to reveal tanned forearms sprinkled with silky black hair and a pile of papers in his hands. The total surprise on his face was unmistakable, and Beth wondered whether it was at finding Helena leaning so menacingly towards her or at finding Helena there at all.

'What's going on?' His deep voice cracked through the electricity tearing a path in the air between the two women, and Helena leapt back, clutching the remnants of her composure to herself. Beth had to applaud the fast recovery she made as she bestowed a forced smile on Dominic, while waving a placatory hand toward Beth.

'I was just examining the changes in *your* Dr Anderson,' she explained almost off-handedly, although neither of them missed the emphasis on the pronoun. 'It really is remarkable!'

'Remarkable,' repeated Dominic, his voice and face carefully neutral.

Taking this as encouragement, coupled with the fact that after one quick glance at Beth Dominic was ignoring her, Helena was emboldened to continue. 'We were discussing why she had undergone such a. . .remarkable. . . makeover.'

'Really?' Dominic's voice still sounded neutral but the gleam in his eyes told Beth that his temper had moved up a gear. That increased her discomfort as she wasn't sure who he was angry with, or why.

'It had to be something important to go to all that effort.' Helena was going to drag this out as long as possible, Beth realised, knowing how embarrassed she would be.

'I don't think. . .' she began, but neither of the others was listening to her.

'I thought butterflies emerged naturally,' Beth heard Dominic say smoothly, and recognised with something like shock that he was going to stand up for her. Which could only mean that Helena was the target of his anger. But apparently the other woman didn't read the same signals.

'Very chivalrous, Dominic,' Helena laughed, the sound a trifle forced, 'but we all know there's more to it than that, don't we?' She turned to include Beth in her statement. 'Beth here decided that if she was ever going to catch you for a husband she needed to brush up her image—look more suitable to be your wife. The quietly adoring act wasn't getting her anywhere, was it?'

The gasp from Beth sounded unnaturally loud in the ensuing silence and, try as she might, no sound would come out to deny the words.

Dominic's eyes flicked briefly to Beth but then settled back on Helena, their deep blue shading into hard black granite although his mouth was smiling deceptively. 'Now there's a thought,' he said conversationally, and looked back at Beth, his expression softening fractionally as he did so. 'In fact, now that you point it out, Beth would make an excellent wife.'

'What?' Both women spoke together but Helena's strident tone drowned out Beth's anguished cry, and it was the former to whom Dominic turned.

'We've worked together for years now and we get along reasonably well. Beth's an excellent psychiatrist and, as you say, she now looks spectacular. Altogether, not a bad idea. Thank you for suggesting it.'

'Now look here. . .' But no one was looking, or listening, to Beth.

Recovering fast from her shock, Helena got in her last, unkind dig. 'And, of course, she loves you.'

'What?' Now it was Dominic's turn to look thoroughly shaken.

'Certainly she does. She has for years. Why else try to attract your attention in this way?'

Beth felt the blood rush to her face before it immediately receded, leaving her ashen as she went into shock. Knowing it to be impossible, she didn't even try to speak. Dazedly she knew that Dominic was giving her a very strange look but still she couldn't do—or say—anything. The shocking truth was being borne home to her. Helena Graham was right! She did love Dominic! It *was* the main reason for her transformation. . . Dear God, she thought, what a way to find out. And what did she do now?

'Whoever Beth loves is a very lucky man,' she dimly heard Dominic telling Helena, his voice almost gentle, 'but that man isn't me.'

'Dominic, you're being blind. . .' Helena sounded less sure of herself, confused by Dominic's attitude and soft voice. A softness which was dropped as swiftly as it had been taken up.

'You're the one who is blind, Helena. I've tried letting you down lightly but you won't see what I've been trying to tell you for weeks. So I'll spell it out for you. We're through. I don't want to see you again. Now I suggest you leave.'

'Dominic—'

'Now!'

As though she finally accepted that she had overplayed her hand once too often and had ignominiously lost, Helena marched to the stairs, turning round at the last moment. 'I hope you're very happy together. You deserve one another.' The words, sounding more like a threat than a blessing, hung in the air even as it reverberated from the slammed door as she exited the building.

The sound galvanised Beth into action and she made to run but Dominic caught her in her office, holding her body close to his, his grip on her upper arms too tight for her to wriggle away from him.

'No, Beth, don't run away.' His voice sounded softer, more compassionate than she could ever remember having heard it. 'Let's talk about it. Let's get the embarrassment over with. I'm sorry you had to go through that, but. . .'

'No! I don't. . .'

'We *have* to, Beth,' he insisted, and deep down she knew that he was right. She was hurting and she was embarrassed, but she also knew that if she left now it would be even harder to face him.

'It's not true!' she asserted swiftly, and felt his grip

on her arms tighten before he let her go abruptly to move
away, his back to her.

'What's not true?' he asked quietly, still not looking
at her.

'I don't love you!' she denied, whilst her whole being
was saying, I do, I do. But he must never know that.
Never have the opportunity to laugh at her. Never have
the chance to reject her love, cast it back in her face as
though it were worthless.

'I know that!' The words were clipped, the voice harsh,
but the face he turned to her was his bland, masked,
psychiatrist's face.

'And I didn't change my image because I wanted to
marry you.'

'I know that too.' This time the words sounded more
rueful than anything else. 'Shame!'

'What did you say?' Beth shook her head in disbelief.
Shock must be making her hear things. He couldn't have
said what she thought he had—even as a joke.

'Helena might have been behaving like a first-class
bitch, but she does have a first-class brain. There's something to be said for the idea of us getting married.'

'Dominic! You can't possibly mean that!' Thoroughly
appalled, Beth sank back down into her chair, refusing
to allow herself the briefest daydream that Dominic had
just woken up to the fact that he loved and wanted to
marry her. He was only teasing. But she was too vulnerable to go along with the game. Too late she realised
that her best defence might have been to join the game—
to pretend to examine the idea seriously before laughingly rejecting it. Her shocked reaction was causing
Dominic to regard her with a strange, speculative gleam
in his eye.

'Come, now, Beth,' he was saying, the devilish sparkle
in his eyes belaying the seriousness of his voice. 'Would
marriage to me be so terrible? Everything I said is true.

We've always got along well, despite a few ups and downs. We know each other's worst points, or pretty much. We respect each other. We've survived good times and bad. Am I so unattractive to you that the thought of marriage to me is turning you that very sickly colour?'

Dominic peered hard at her and added in the most conversational tone, as though they were discussing nothing more personal than the weather, 'I've seen some colours in my time but you really are the most peculiar shade of green, Beth.' Dominic's quizzical gaze was not helping her colour, and as her cheeks turned from ashen to rose Dominic grinned, remarking, 'That's better. Pink has to be healthier.' Which had the unfortunate effect of sending Beth well on the way to red.

'Well?' Dominic broke the silence, clearly waiting for an answer to a question which the confused Beth couldn't remember.

'Well, what?' she demanded somewhat belligerently, her temper beginning to override her embarrassment. How dared he do this to her? It was bad enough that Helena Graham saw fit to humiliate her, but there was no need for Dominic to prolong the agony.

'I asked you if I was so unattractive to you that the thought of marriage to me was so totally impossible.'

There was something in Dominic's voice which caused Beth to give him more than the cursory glances she had been bestowing on him for the last few minutes. Although he had the appearance of a man who was treating the matter in a light-hearted way, to Beth's careful scrutiny his act didn't quite ring true. There was a tension about him—in the clenched fist at his side, in the involuntary twitch of a muscle by the corner of his mouth—that told her he wasn't as indifferent to her answer as he might pretend.

And why should he be? she asked herself. He might not be particularly interested in her, but no one wants to

be told that they're totally unattractive—too unattractive
to even consider marrying. About to deny that she found
him in any way attractive, Beth found that she couldn't
do it. The concept of Dominic being vulnerable to her
answer—that he might be feeling insecure—was enough
to push her into telling him the truth—or at least an
edited version of half the truth.

'No, you're not unattractive, Dominic,' she told him
in what she hoped was a matter-of-fact voice, and knew
that she had done the right thing as she saw some of the
tension ease from him, his fist unclenching slowly. But
she couldn't afford to let him think that he was getting
the upper hand. 'However, as we both know, there's a
lot more to marriage than simply finding someone
attractive.'

One of Dominic's finely shaped brows rose at that and
Beth realised that she would be pushing her luck to try
to maintain a worldly-wise position against this man who
knew so graphically that she was not.

'If there wasn't,' she went on doggedly, 'we could
marry any one of a dozen people.'

'Do you find a dozen men attractive, Beth?' Dominic
asked casually, and looked totally taken aback by Beth's
quick, affirmative nod of response. It was almost as
though he had never considered Beth finding anyone
attractive. Beth would have laughed at that if it hadn't
been so tragic. Dominic obviously didn't consider *her*
attractive enough and therefore assumed that she couldn't
be attracted to anyone.

'That doesn't mean to say I'd consider marrying any
of them. And don't try to pretend that there aren't plenty
of women you're attracted to. But would you marry all,
or any, of them?'

Faced with that challenge, there was little Dominic
could do but grin and shrug. 'OK. Point taken. But you're
not going to sidetrack me that easily. Give me one good

reason why we shouldn't get married.'

Why was he persisting? Beth wondered frantically as she searched for some innocuous reply. There had been several opportunities to drop the subject, to change tack, but Dominic kept bringing the conversation back to the one awful topic that Helena had raised.

'Give me one good reason why we should,' she challenged rashly, and as his eyes turned almost black with the sudden widening of his pupils she wished the words unsaid. But it was far too late to call them back.

'Because you're a very beautiful, desirable woman, and I want to make love to you. And I don't think you're going to let me—at least, not without marriage. Are you?' Dominic said the words so casually, in the same matter-of-fact voice that he would have used to ask her if she'd enjoyed her lunch, that it took several seconds for Beth to fully comprehend what he was saying.

As their meaning sank into her numbed brain the colour once again flooded her cheeks. Blood pounded through her veins and she felt herself gasping for breath as she struggled for speech while trying to make sense of what Dominic had said. Did he mean what he was saying? If so, was that supposed to be a proposal? If it wasn't, what was it? And what on earth was she supposed to do?

Taking in Beth's flushed cheeks and wide, confused grey eyes through narrowed eyes, Dominic relaxed his stance and looked more in command both of himself and the situation.

'Well, Beth,' he enquired, almost as though the answer didn't really interest him, 'what's your objection now? Your *good* reason not to marry?'

'We don't love each other,' she said simply, with as much dignity as she could muster. 'And I was brought up to believe that marriage should be based on love.

Without that it's just a hollow sham.'

'And what if one of the partners loves?' Dominic asked gently, his voice held under rigid control and his eyes never leaving her face.

Beth gasped and turned away, pain lancing through her. He couldn't know how she felt about him, could he? Was he still trying to find out if Helena's accusation had been true? But why? He wasn't a cruel man, and if he truly thought she loved him he wouldn't play this unkind game with her. But what else could he be getting at? She had to answer him. She couldn't leave the unspoken accusation hanging in the air.

'It's not enough,' she told him finally, when the silence became harder to bear than answering, her voice commendably steady. 'If only one person loves it will eventually turn to resentment when it's not returned, and that will lead to misery for both.'

'You don't think one person's love can carry both?' Dominic's quietly voiced question caused Beth more anguish. That was what she wanted to believe, of course it was, but she wasn't sure that it was the truth. There was the other person's side, too.

Slowly shaking her head, she replied, unable to look at him, 'No. In time I think it would become too much of a burden. Knowing someone loved you and that you didn't return it would become a noose round that person's neck. They would eventually want to shake free of feelings they couldn't return.'

As she spoke she could feel the edges of her composure begin to crumble. It was a miracle she had withstood the strain as long as she had, but now she had to get away from Dominic before she gave way altogether.

'Wise Bethesda.' Dominic's voice sounded faint, as though she were hearing it from a great distance. 'You were aptly named. Mercy exists in not allowing false hopes.' With that he swung away from her and dis-

appeared into his office, shutting the door quietly—but
with a sense of finality—behind him.

Somehow she got through the rest of the day but as she
let herself into the safe haven of her flat the emotions
which had barely been held in check overwhelmed her
and tears coursed down her face. How could she have
been so blindly stupid not to have known that she loved
Dominic?

Why else had the thought of leaving him caused her
so much distress? Why else did she never approve of his
girlfriends? Why else had she allowed him to walk all
over her all these years, and then changed when she
thought that was what he wanted?

As the last thought surfaced in the grey mire of her
misery she forced herself to stand back and take stock.
The last statement wasn't completely true. *She* had
wanted to change, and she had set about the transformation as much for her own sake as because it was what
she thought Dominic wanted. She mustn't forget that.
She was grateful for whatever had pushed her into the
transformation. These positive changes would stay with
her, whatever happened in the future.

Rubbing her eyes to banish the tears, she stumbled
into the bathroom to view the ravages the storm of weep-
ing had caused. So much for a butterfly, she admonished
herself. At the moment she more closely resembled a
caterpillar—and a squashed one at that! The gory picture
that conjured up was enough to spur her into repairing
the damage caused by blotchy skin, red-rimmed eyes and
smudged mascara.

It was as she was packing her bag for the brief journey
north that she remembered that Dominic had called her
Bethesda. His comment about mercy indicated that he
knew the meaning of her name. One of the meanings
was 'house of mercy'. She gave an inelegant sniff as her

eyes filled with tears again at the thought of Dominic
making the effort to look up her name. Another sniff was
halted as she remembered the other meaning of her name,
'house of the stream', after a pool in Jerusalem which
was remarkable for the sudden intermittent flow of its
waters.

She suppressed a chuckle as a wave of hysteria washed
over her. If her crying bout couldn't be described as a
sudden flow of water forming a pool, what could? Truly,
she was well named. But in the midst of her misery she
couldn't help but take comfort from the fact that, for
whatever reason, Dominic had cared enough to find out
about her unusual name.

'I went to see Bill Sullivan.' Beth dropped the words
into the silence which had accompanied the last half-hour
of the journey. Early casual conversation had petered out
and she wanted to do something to shake up Dominic.

'You did what?' The car lurched as Dominic momentarily put his foot down, before controlling his reflexes.
When Beth didn't say anything he was forced to add in
a more moderate tone, 'Why?'

'I just wanted to see him again. I suppose I had some
idea of confronting him,' she confessed, 'to set my mind
at rest. It's OK, I didn't,' she reassured him quickly, then
proceeded to fill him in on the details of the meeting.

'And now?'

'Now. . .' She sighed. 'I accept that it's unlikely that
Mr Sullivan was beating his wife. There's no evidence.'

'Is that it? No evidence, rather than you believe he
did nothing?'

'I didn't ask him but, no, I don't believe he was beating
his wife.'

'I'm glad to hear it.' Dominic sounded serious.

'Why?'

'I was worried that you were showing a prejudice

against him simply because he was a man.'

'No. But I was trying to listen to a patient.'

'Point taken.'

'I should add that I did some checking on Martha Bell.'

'And?'

'And it seems that this isn't the first husband she had accused of beating up his wife with no evidence.'

'Ah!' Beth could hear the smile in his voice.

'Don't say it!' she warned.

'I wasn't going to.'

'Hmm.'

'And who do you feel most sorry for now?'

'Jenny,' was her quick reply. 'I've always felt sorry for her.'

'Why?'

Beth shrugged. 'Maybe because she always sounded so downtrodden. And she was. Battered into despair by the people who loved her and couldn't meet each other halfway.'

'Yes.' The chill in Dominic's voice caused her to glance at him and she saw his mouth tighten. 'I guess I was lucky. My wife decided to side with her parents and divorce me.'

'Oh.' Beth desperately wanted to know more but didn't know how to ask. She didn't need to.

'My in-laws opposed our marrying, and it turned out that they were right.'

'They couldn't have objected to you being a doctor, surely?'

'A doctor, no. A junior house officer—yes. We were young, in love and blind to the reality of the next few years. We married a week after I graduated. It was a disaster.

'Looking back, I can't believe we were that naïve. I hadn't realised how. . .young. . .Clara was. Nor how few resources she had. She hated being left on her own so much. It got a bit better after the first couple of years but then I had to start studying again for my membership exams. You know how it is. She found someone else.'

'I'm sorry.'

'Don't be. I'm not. She's happily married now to someone else. It was a bit strange at the time, my wife going off with my boss, but I got used to it.'

Beth gasped, but Dominic just grinned.

'Mummy and Daddy weren't overly impressed with him, either. Too old. But that was what Clara needed. An older man, from a wealthy background, who could indulge her. The money made up for the time he couldn't always spend with her.'

Beth risked another glance at him and he took his eyes briefly from the road to smile at her. Unaccountably relieved, she smiled back. Relaxing, Beth wasn't prepared for his next words.

'But what about you? Why aren't you married?'

Colour flooded her cheeks and Beth knew that she had to answer. But how could she explain something she didn't really understand herself?

'I'm not sure. When I was young I was very shy and didn't socialise much. Then I started filling my time doing schoolwork. I got a lot of praise for that and work just became a habit. I went out with one or two people, nothing serious, but long hours and more study always seemed to get in the way. Now I'm used to my life as it is.' She hoped that sounded plausible without sounding too pathetic.

'You sound as though you're happy with your life.'

'I'm not unhappy,' she prevaricated.

'Don't you want to be married? Have children?'

'Only if I loved someone,' she replied, adding silently, And if he loved me, as she shut her eyes to the picture of miniature Dominics crowded round her.

*   *   *

It had been a wasted journey, Beth was sure of that. The junior doctor on duty had been more than a little surprised to be confronted by two members of the Commission in the middle of the evening, demanding to be shown around the hospital, but had, nevertheless, taken their appearance in his stride and had escorted them to the admission wards.

Old, grey Victorian wards were not inspiring at the best of times, but Beth noted that some attempt had been made to give them a more homey touch and the partitioning which had been installed gave a measure of privacy. It was by no means great, but it could have been worse.

Since the big psychiatric hospitals were being run down with the advent of the care in the community policy, much of the hospital accommodation had been left to deteriorate, the view being that since the beds would close eventually there was little to be gained from maintaining them.

'I want to see the locked ward.' Dominic sounded most reasonable, which Beth knew to be a sign that he was expecting trouble and that he would face it head-on.

'I think I should call out Dr McCann. It would be better if he took you round.'

'I think not.' Dominic's voice brooked no argument but it was clear to both of them that the young doctor was less than happy with the request. 'By all means call him, but *after* you have shown us to the locked ward.'

Beth found it in her heart to feel sorry for the young man, caught in the middle of what was clearly going to be a difficult situation, but he delivered them to the locked ward. There were very few patients there and those who were, were either there as a result of a court order, detention under part of the Mental Health Act or had been behaving violently and required a controlled and contained space.

One look at the nurse in charge told Beth that she didn't trust him an inch. It wasn't just that he was overweight with lank, greasy hair, but there was an air of menace about him that seemed to sit ill on someone in a caring role. His civility was touched with a surliness which had Beth standing that bit closer to Dominic. Andy McGregor was not a man Beth wished to spend much time with.

Bracing herself, she reminded herself that this was her job and that she hadn't had problems before and that she was well trained to manage people with difficult behaviour, whether they were patients or staff.

'Seen enough?' The brief tour of the ward had told them little. They had spoken to a few patients but the nurse had always been in earshot.

'I want to talk to you.' A slight man approached Dominic and stood squarely in front of him.

'Not now, Malcolm.' The burly nurse moved to the patient's side, his bulk serving to emphasise the apparent slenderness of the other man. Casting a critical eye over him, Beth noted that his air of slightness was something of an illusion and that beneath the thin T-shirt were well-defined muscles.

'Why not?' The tone might have been taken as aggressive but Beth preferred to think of it as determined. 'I've something to say to these doctors. Something they should know.'

'I said, not now!' There was no mistaking the belligerence in the nurse's voice and Beth tensed. Dominic laid a reassuring hand on her arm, as if checking any intervention she might have made but also moving her slightly behind him.

The two men focused their attention on Dominic who, to Beth's concerned eyes, seemed to grow in size and stature as gradually all eyes in the ward were drawn to the mismatched quartet. The tension was thick and heavy, holding the men in a fog of palpable anger and resentment.

'I think if Mr. . .' Dominic stopped and raised an eyebrow, waiting for one of the two men to supply him with a name. It was the patient who broke the silence.

'Paterson. Malcolm Paterson.' He stuck out his hand and had it firmly grasped by Dominic, who completed the introductions. 'I'm Dominic Farquhar and this is Dr Beth Anderson. We are from the—'

'The Commission. Aye, I know that. And about bloody time, if you don't mind my saying so.'

'Not at all.' Dominic smiled and, watching him, Beth could almost see him turn up the volume on the controls marked charm, reassurance and authority. Malcolm Paterson visibly relaxed and the tension in the ward came down a notch or two.

'Maybe we could use your office briefly?' Dominic turned to Andy McGregor, his expression leaving the nurse little option but to comply.

As Beth turned with the two men towards the nurse's office Malcolm Paterson stopped, his faded blue eyes wary as he raked her from head to toe. 'Not you, hen. This is men's business. No offence.'

'None taken,' Beth replied coolly, speaking quickly to get in before Dominic could intervene. She didn't want him speaking on her behalf and weakening her position, and even less did she want him agreeing with Mr Paterson. 'But this is Commission business, and I *am* a member of the Commission.'

That seemed to stop Malcolm Paterson dead in his tracks as his eyes hardened for a second as they ran over her a second time. What he saw must have reassured him for he nodded briefly. Holding his pale gaze steadily, Beth continued softly but firmly, 'And you might find it useful to have two people listen to what you have to say.'

The tone of her voice must have reached Malcolm and

he understood her underlying meaning for a wide grin split his face, albeit briefly, changing his appearance dramatically and taking years off his hard image. 'Aye, that it might. Come along, then.' He stood aside to let Beth precede him towards the office.

As she passed Dominic she saw one well-shaped eyebrow ascend heavenwards but he said nothing. Beth didn't miss the twitch of his lips, however, and was annoyed that he could be amused by the interchange. She wanted his approval, his support. Amusement made her feel like a child being humoured.

They had barely seated themselves when Malcolm launched into a litany of complaints about the way patients were treated. They let him run on for a while to get his pent-up anger out, then Dominic threw in one or two questions.

'The main thrust of your complaint, then, is regarding Mr McGregor?'

'Aye. The man's a bully. Worse than a bully, he's a thug. He has a vicious temper which he takes out on patients. Staff, too, sometimes. I've heard him tear a strip off some of the junior nurses, the young lasses. And he doesn't care who hears. He taunts patients all the time. A couple of the men are married and he goes on about what their wives are up to while they're stuck in here. Drives them to the edge, he does. Anyone shows any sign of weakness, and he's there ready to exploit it.'

'And you say he threatens patients and has been violent to them.'

'Aye.'

'Can you prove it?' Both pairs of eyes turned to Beth, as though they had forgotten she was there. She held her ground. 'At the moment it would be your word against his. Will anyone one else support you?'

There was a moment's silence while the question hung in the air, and Beth wondered if they had made a mistake.

'Aye, they'll confirm what I've said if they know he'll no be back. Otherwise they'll be too frightened to talk because of reprisals.'

'Have you complained before, then?'

'Aye, many times. To Dr McCann. To management. Turned a blind eye. Don't want to be bothered, and not about to take the word of a bunch of loonies.'

They were nearing the hospital entrance when a figure darted out from a darkened doorway. Looking almost comically furtive but genuinely agitated, the man introduced himself as Dr Simon Barr, a registrar. 'I wonder if it's possible to have a meeting with you tomorrow,' he asked hesitantly.

Neither Beth nor Dominic was surprised by his request. There was evidently something on his mind. 'Certainly,' Dominic responded smoothly. 'Ten o'clock all right?'

'Yes, thanks. Fine.' He stumbled to a halt but obviously had more to say. 'I. . .er. . .I . . .phoned Donald Gordon. He's the charge nurse. He wants a formal meeting with you tomorrow as well.'

Dominic's eyebrows twitched, but didn't ascend into his hairline as Beth's were doing. 'That would be helpful, no doubt. We'll arrange to see him in the morning,' Dominic confirmed.

'I'll meet you in the bar in fifteen minutes.' They had checked into a small hotel a short drive from the hospital and were making their way to their rooms. Stopping by her door, Beth nodded her agreement, conscious that Dominic was stopping at the room next door.

By unspoken mutual consent the journey from the hospital had been made in virtual silence, the only observations being made about directions and referral to the map. They both needed some space to think about what they had been told and then uninterrupted time to discuss it. That couldn't be done while navigating the narrow roads, sudden tight bends and less than clear directions to the hotel.

'Well?' Dominic voiced the question as they sat at a small table tucked away in a dark corner of the tiny bar, a plate of sandwiches and two cups of coffee before them. Dominic had succumbed to the persuasions of the proprietor and was nursing a malt whisky from the extensive range lined up behind the bar. He took a sip and gave an appreciative sigh, before putting the glass down.

'We had better get business dealt with before I give my full attention to this and enjoy it as it deserves.' He pushed the glass to one side and returned his attention to Beth. 'Well?' he repeated.

'You were right,' Beth confirmed immediately. 'The rumours had something in them.'

'You believed Malcolm Paterson, then?' Dominic sounded mildly surprised, which threw Beth into total confusion. It hadn't crossed her mind that the litany of complaints and accusations about harassment and unfair and brutal treatment were anything but true.

'Yes, of course. Didn't you?' Had she missed something? she wondered as she mentally replayed the interview. Had Dominic picked up on something she had overlooked? Was she jumping to hasty conclusions simply because she had taken an instant dislike to Andy McGregor? The thought brought her up sharply, emphasising a distinct lack of professionalism and a lack of objectivity which she was usually so careful to maintain. She mustn't make the same mistake she had in believing Martha about Jenny.

Dominic didn't reply at once but let the silence hang between them, building the tension. Beth felt worse by the second. Colour washed through her cheeks as she became convinced that she had overlooked something both vital and obvious. Dominic obviously thought the man was lying. What could she have missed? Just as she was going to have to justify herself, Dominic spoke.

'Actually, I did. What I was wondering was why nothing has been done before.'

Beth let out a held-in breath and relaxed. 'That crossed my mind, too.'

'I'll admit that at first I was sceptical about the extent of the problem,' Dominic explained, 'but there was something compelling about Malcolm's story. Even if there is some exaggeration there is a clear need for a full investigation.'

'Yes.' Beth's reply was hesitant.

'We have to hear both sides of the story, Beth, you know that. I'll go so far as to admit that I believe McGregor has used some untoward force, but the man must have the opportunity to put his case before you judge him.'

'You don't think we should have asked for Mr McGregor's suspension from duty?' Beth voiced the doubt which had been with her since listening to Malcolm Paterson's story. Procedures in most hospitals had been tightened up—many thought too far and unfairly—against nurses, but it was common for a nurse to be suspended on pay, pending an inquiry, when serious allegations had been made against him or her.

Although Dominic shrugged, his frown deepened. 'Maybe. But it seemed a bit melodramatic. We can get that done tomorrow.'

With that Beth had to be satisfied, although the nagging sense of unease lingered as they discussed their plans for the next day.

Feeling perfectly at ease with Dominic while they talked about work, it was only as they started up the stairs towards their rooms that Beth's attention was drawn back to the tensions in their personal relationship.

Immediately she felt her body stiffen, tension coiling her nerves tightly and causing her to move away from the suddenly overwhelmingly male presence at her side. A quick glance through half-closed lashes showed Dominic apparently unconcerned and totally at ease. Clearly their relative isolation, tucked away in this tiny Highland hotel, was not causing him any anxieties. Berating herself for being so foolish, Beth stopped outside her bedroom door.

Dominic carried on for a few steps before he realised that Beth was no longer with him. Stopping abruptly, he swung round to face her and Beth saw her tension mirrored in his face. He took the two steps back to her and stood facing her, as though suddenly unsure what his next action should be.

'Goodnight, Dominic see you in the morning.' Beth was proud of her calm voice uttering the banal words.

Dominic relaxed visibly, a slow, sexy smile twisting both his lips and Beth's heart, but all he did was lean forward and brush a gentle kiss across her lips.

'Goodnight, sweet Bethesda.' Then he was turning away and heading towards his room without a backward glance.

Beth entered her room and shut the door quietly, before letting out her breath. It was getting harder and harder to maintain a professional distance with Dominic. Her very limited experience with men left her uncertain how to proceed.

CHAPTER SEVEN

'BETH. Beth!'

Beth burrowed further into the covers, the voice that was insistently calling her name mingling with a loud thudding sound and neither sitting comfortably in the dream she was having. A dream in which Dominic was whispering sweet nothings in her ear, while at the same time his hands were creating sweet sensations as they travelled across her body.

'Beth. Wake up!'

She catapulted upright in bed as the hands which had been caressing her so softly in her dream now held her shoulders firmly and shook her awake. 'What—?' she began, her befuddled brain only taking in that Dominic was standing by the side of her bed. One look at his worried face, however, convinced her that this was no lovers' tryst. Whatever had brought Dominic to her room in the middle of the night, neither love nor lust was on the agenda.

'Get dressed and meet me downstairs.' He was halfway across the room as he issued his orders, satisfied now that she was properly awake.

'Why?' She seemed incapable of more than one word utterances at the moment.

Dominic's steps didn't falter, not did he look back. 'I'll explain in the car. Simon Barr phoned.' With that he was out of the door, leaving Beth to scramble into her clothes.

'What happened?' Beth clutched at the dashboard as Dominic swung the car slightly too fast round the tight

bend in the narrow road. In the pitch black of the
Highland night the curves in the road appeared out of
nowhere. Although clear, the few stars frosting the navy-
blue sky gave no real light and the moon was nowhere
in sight. Another tight bend had Dominic muttering under
his breath as he braked, but from then on he took the
winding road at a more steady pace.

'Simon Barr phoned in something of a state. Said that
a fight had broken out on the ward between, as far as I
can make out, McGregor and Paterson. Several of the
other patients joined in. I'm not sure who raised the alarm
but it seems to have become a bit of a free-for-all.'
His full lips tightened with anger. 'It should never have
happened.' The words were bitten out and Beth watched
as his grip tightened on the steering-wheel, his knuckles
whitening. 'I should have seen it coming.'

It was only then that Beth realised how much of his
reined-in anger was directed at himself, and she understood exactly how he felt. She, too, felt that they should
have been able to prevent this outburst occurring. A new
thought struck her. 'Why did Simon Barr phone you?'

'Don't be more naïve than you have to be.' Dominic
didn't look at her as he spoke but Beth was left in no
doubt of his irritation with her. Of course she wasn't so
naïve as not to spot the immediate implications of the
young doctor's phone call, but what she had really been
asking was exactly what Simon Barr had said. She had
no intention of satisfying Dominic by spelling that out.

By now they were nearly at the hospital, and as they
drove up to the impressive gateway of the main entrance
Dominic spoke again.

'Sorry, Beth. I shouldn't take my frustrations with this
case out on you.' He drew a long, steadying breath—
almost, Beth thought, as though calming himself before
moving into the fray that awaited them.

'Has he called Dr McCann?' That had been the question she had wanted to ask earlier, and she was relieved when Dominic nodded.

'Yes. I checked that. It would have been far too awkward had he not.'

Simon Barr was waiting and hurried them towards the ward. Far from the scene of carnage that Beth had expected, the ward was comparatively quiet, with a couple of groups of men sitting drinking mugs of tea. A young female nurse was talking quietly with an agitated man twice her size, but even an untrained eye would have spotted that he was responding to her calm manner and trained approach.

Another group of three men, all still visibly agitated, were clustered in the corner, a tall, thin man at their centre the focus of their attention. Seeing the new party entering the ward, he moved towards them and introduced himself as Donald Gordon, the charge nurse for the ward. The look that flashed between him and Simon Barr showed who had called him out. The young doctor had obviously been very busy on the telephone.

'It's good to have you here, Dr Farquhar. And you, Dr Anderson.' His smile showed genuine warmth but there was still a wariness in his eyes and a tension in the lines of his jaw. Both Beth and Dominic shook his hand, silently acknowledging the charge nurse's authority over his ward. 'Everything is very much under control now, as you can see.' Even as he spoke the large man and the diminutive nurse were helping themselves to tea and joining one of the seated groups. 'Will you be wanting to take statements from people now?'

'If you think that appropriate, certainly,' Dominic agreed. 'It would be helpful from the principals at least. The rest can wait until morning.'

'Good.' Donald Gordon's quick nod and fleeting smile indicated his approval of the plan. 'One of you can use my office and—' A noise by the door cut him off and alerted them to the entrance of a newcomer.

'Dr McCann.' Donald Gordon's quietly breathed comment confirmed Beth's suspicions as to who the portly newcomer was.

Dominic, having previously met the older doctor, went to greet him and Beth, along with the others, was immediately aware of the tension between the two men. A hurried, quiet conversation had Beth worried as to what was going on and what was being cooked up between them. Watching Dominic's back, his increasing tension was apparent and she wondered if she should interfere.

Softly spoken as the words were, the tightly suppressed anger was evident. 'We don't need your interference, Dr Farquhar. I am quite capable of dealing with this matter myself.'

'I would not dispute that, but in this case—'

'The hospital authorities will be informed and appropriate action taken.' Dr McCann spoke over Dominic, carrying on as though the younger man hadn't said anything.

'That's all very well, but—' Again Dominic was ignored.

'Everything is under control. We don't need your involvement.' Beth noted that Dr McCann was modifying his force and language in an attempt to mollify Dominic, but it wasn't working. If anything, it was making matters worse.

'It's too late for that.' This time there was no mistaking the intent in Dominic's voice. 'We already have a complaint made by a patient against a nurse, which will require investigation. The complaint also includes the mishandling of previous complaints by the hospital authorities.' Dr McCann paled at that, Beth noted, his thin lips pressing tightly together as though to choke back the words he longed to utter. 'Like it or not, Dr McCann, we *are* involved.'

As during the afternoon, Dominic elected for Beth to
interview Malcolm Paterson with him. They would then
both see Andy McGregor, the nurse. All the other inter-
views could be left to the next day.

Malcolm came in, looking a good deal more composed
than might have been expected given the circumstances.
His cheek was swollen and there were the beginnings of
a bruise around his eye, but otherwise he seemed to be
a reasonable shape. His story was fairly straightforward.

'He wanted to know what I had said to you,' Malcolm
told them, 'and I told him it was none of his business.
Well, he didn't like that and kept insisting.' He smiled
at the memory. 'No way was I going to tell him.' The
smile grew broader. 'Then I thought, hell, why not? He's
going to find out some time. So I told him I was making
a formal complaint against him and the way he pushes
and shoves us around all the time. Not to mention the
couple of times he's really lost control.'

He looked positively smug by now. 'Anyway, he
went—' he stopped suddenly, casting a quick glance
at Beth and obviously deciding to modify his language
—berserk. Lunged for me. He caught me off guard and
I went down. He was sitting on my chest and punching
me when the others in the ward piled in, trying to pull
him off me.' He ran a hand across his torso. 'He's a big
man to have sitting on your chest, I can tell you!'

Comparing the relative sizes of the two men, Beth
shuddered. Andy McGregor could easily have done serious damage.

There was more in a similar vein but the story
remained fundamentally the same. The interview with
Andy McGregor essentially corroborated the outline but
differed over the details.

'Me—attack? No way. Paterson went for me and I
had to defend myself.'

'Mr Paterson says you sat on his chest ar
punched him.'

'Aye, well. . .I sat on him to keep him under contr
until someone could sedate him, but punch him-
no way.'

Since immediate suspension was the only response
any complaint of violence which was initiated, the
would need to be a full inquiry.

In the car Beth was deep in thought but Dominic wasn
going to let her remain lost in an inner world. 'Well,' k
demanded as he eased the car through the hospital gate
'first impressions?'

'He set him up.'

'Absolutely! But that doesn't excuse McGregor
behaviour.'

'I wasn't for a moment suggesting that it did,' Be
replied, stung. Why did Dominic always misjudge he
'Just that it was probably the only way he thought k
could prove his case.'

'Hmm.' Dominic's attention was momentarily mo
on the road than Beth but was soon back with her. 'In
way I feel sorry for McGregor.'

'What?' Beth was aghast. It was the last thing she ha
expected Dominic to say.

'Don't worry, I'm not excusing his behaviour. The
is no excuse for violence. But he's got a difficult job ar
he's not properly trained for it. The hospital manageme
is partly to blame. There should have been more staff c
a ward like that, even at night, and certainly someor
with more training and experience.'

'Yes.' He was right, much as Beth didn't want to adm
it. 'So now what?'

'I think we initiate a full-scale report into the runnir
of the ward and as much of the hospital as we can impk
cate, that's what!' Dominic said with some satisfactio

'But that will have to wait until we get back to Glasgow. *Now*—' he placed heavy emphasis on the word '—the rest of the night is ours.'

Beth felt the colour flood her face and she was entirely speechless. The low chuckle from Dominic did nothing to calm her tumultuous feelings which were suddenly raging totally out of control. Did he mean what she thought he meant? And, if so, what was she going to do about it?

When Dominic did nothing more than wish her sweet dreams as he said goodnight and headed for his room, Beth didn't know whether to be relieved or disappointed. Two hours later, unable to sleep and lying wide-eyed and restless, she knew she was disappointed.

Unsettled summer weather gave way to even more unsettled autumn weather and Beth's emotions followed suit. Her usual calm acceptance of life was being sorely tried by Dominic's changing moods, which ranged from warm and sunny one moment to distinctly stormy the next. Talking things over with Morven helped her to see the problems more clearly. She was less partisan than Cassie.

'I don't understand. He was positively chirpy on the trip back from the Highland, and for the next few days.'

'You saw a lot of him?'

'Yes. We were setting up an inquiry.' Since Dr Barr and Mr Gordon had been prepared to make statements both about Andy McGregor and management's refusal to deal with the situation things were moving quickly, but she couldn't tell Morven that.

'And then?'

'And then things changed.'

'Why?'

'I don't know.'

'How did you act? Before things changed?'

'Fine. I think. Well, if I'm honest, I didn't really know what I thought or felt about Dominic by then. Seeing him all the time didn't help so I began to back off.'

'There you are, then!' Morven was triumphant. 'Of course the man is moody when you start cooling towards him.'

'Sometimes when we're working together he's charming and fun, more considerate than I would have believed possible. I'm comfortable with him then but sometimes, with no warning at all, he snaps, challenges what I'm doing and goes off in a—there's no other word for it— sulk.' Beth nibbled at her lower lip. 'If I knew what triggered his moods maybe I could forestall them. At the very least I would know when they were coming.'

'Maybe it's something you're doing.'

'And maybe it's not. Maybe he's just fed up with me.'

Morven grinned. 'And maybe he's not. Maybe it's frustration.'

'Why the deep sighs, Beth?'

Her heart gave a thud as Dominic spoke behind her. His silent entry into the small kitchen at the Commission had gone unnoticed by her and she gave a guilty jump, having been staring out of the window for the best part of ten minutes while she waited for the kettle to boil and reviewed her feelings for Dominic. Apparently, she had also been sighing.

Unable to summon up more than a shrug by way of response, she was aware that Dominic was giving her a very calculated look before he backed out without saying another word.

As so often of late, she wondered how much longer she could go on working with him. Since the moment of revelation, when she had faced up to her love for Dominic, she had discovered hitherto unknown powers of ignoring what she could not deal with. For most of the time she was able to push this new, disturbing insight into her emotions into the recesses of her anxious mind.

It was only on rare occasions that she let herself remember, let herself feel. Since the consequence of such times was usually that she ended up crying herself to sleep, she thought it wisest to limit them. Insofar as she was able. And somehow, miraculously, she could.

At least, up until now. It was inevitable that sometimes she let her thoughts drift into a fantasy future when Dominic would realise that he loved her, too, and it all ended happily ever after. Even so, she recognised that if she was to retain her sanity she couldn't indulge in such dreams often. And never while she was at work. So far she had managed, but it was getting harder and harder. Dominic's mood swings didn't help.

The idea that she could leave—get another job—brushed the fringes of her awareness and was immediately banished. There was no way she could contemplate leaving Dominic. One day in the future when she could no longer push her feelings away but could not live with them either she would have to face reality and leave. But not until then. Or the other, awful possibility.

Beth knew without a shadow of a doubt that when Dominic announced his engagement, as he inevitably would, she would leave and head for new horizons. But the cutting pain shooting through her at the idea of Dominic married was enough for her to push those thoughts aside, too.

'Still sighing, Beth?' Dominic was back again, clutching a mug and heading for the kettle, his expression both quizzical and amused. Beth wasn't best pleased to be found still daydreaming, and with a visible effort tried to pull herself together.

'I was thinking about my MD and the future,' she told him, which was not a total fabrication. If she was going to leave then anything which would improve her prospects had to be seriously considered.

The amusement was wiped from Dominic's face at her words, his brows drawing together in the semblance of a frown, and Beth wondered uneasily if he could read her mind.

'Not thinking of leaving me, are you, Beth?' he asked quietly, too quietly for her liking. 'That wouldn't do at all. I need you here.'

If only that were true, she thought wistfully, while the word 'why?' hovered on her lips. Fortunately neither thought was spoken and she shook her head, her eyes widening as his scowl disappeared and he looked pleased with himself once more.

'Don't even think it,' he admonished her softly, before leaving her pondering exactly what he'd meant.

'Goodbye, Robert.' Beth laughed, a soft, gently intimate sound, then repeated her farewell into the phone—this time to Cassie—just as the door slammed. Dominic was watching her, a truly furious expression on his face.

'So, Robert is still around, is he?' The words were snarled out, flung vaguely in Beth's direction. She was still sitting with the telephone receiver in her hand, caught almost in a moment of suspended animation as Dominic advanced on her before she broke the hypnotic spell of his eyes and fumbled the receiver back into place.

Still Dominic kept coming and only stopped when he was right up to Beth's desk, at which point he leant forward across it with his braced arms supporting his body as he pushed his still-scowling face close to hers. From such confined quarters the fire in the depths of his eyes seemed to give them an almost purple haze, and to Beth it felt as though sparks were flying from them and landing on her skin—her whole body warming from his, ready to ignite.

As the musky scent of his aftershave assailed her nostrils she gave an imperceptible shake of her head and tried to move away. But without making it obvious that she was moving her chair, there was nothing she could do, nowhere she could go. Turning her head slightly so that she didn't have to meet his eyes, Beth was disconcerted to find Dominic's warm breath on her cheek.

'Look at me, Beth,' he commanded, and when she stubbornly refused he reiterated more softly, '*Look* at me, Bethesda.' The caressing quality of his voice and the use of her full name drew her eyes to him, and when she finally raised her head to meet his gaze she was further confounded by the expression she found there.

The blazing anger which had been so dominant was banked down, but the almost tender expression replacing it was something Beth couldn't fully comprehend.

'What do you want, Dominic?' Beth struggled to keep her voice on an even keel and was feeling pleased with her control until she saw the glimmer of amusement crossing Dominic's face, which told her that she hadn't sounded quite as disinterested, or in control, as she had thought.

'Tell me about this Robert,' Dominic invited, putting Beth in something of a dilemma.

She didn't understand why he was so interested but if she told him the truth, that Robert was her godson, this apparent interest he had would be squashed once and for all. On the other hand, she quite liked the idea of Robert giving her some protection. If Dominic continued to believe that she was interested in another man he wouldn't enquire into her feelings for him. His apparent jealousy of Robert she couldn't believe was personal but more a reflection of his resentment of anything which took her attention away from her work and—indirectly—from him.

'There's nothing to tell, really. . .' she began, her voice trailing away as the lines between his brows, which had almost disappeared, creased into existence again as his scowl became more pronounced.

'Tell me and I'll decide whether it's nothing or not,' he said, his voice—bordering on indifference—belaying the expression in his eyes.

'You don't understand about Robert. . .' Beth tried again, wondering how Dominic would react to being told that Robert was an infant of a few months old. Would he feel that she had deliberately set out to deceive him, or try to make a fool of him?

Straightening from his position, Dominic folded his arms across his chest and fixed her with a look that had turned frighteningly icy.

'Are you planning to marry him?' he demanded, catching her off guard enough for her to utter a single, simple negative. At his raised eyebrows, she was forced to add an explanation.

'You've got it all wrong. . .'

'Have I?' he queried. 'I'm not sure I like the sound of this. . .relationship, Beth. Although I must say I'm glad to see you have the sense to realise you can't marry this man.'

'I'll marry who I like!' Beth found herself goaded into defying Dominic rather than explaining who Robert was.

'You think so?' Dominic's smile was one of masked anger. 'I'm still waiting to hear your "good reason" for not marrying me.' The words hung in the air between them, leaving Beth totally dumbfounded and unable to do anything but stare at Dominic in something approaching horror. She had hoped—prayed—that Dominic had forgotten that awful conversation but here he was making himself sound like the aggrieved party, as though he had really proposed to her and she had heartlessly turned him down.

How dared he? she asked herself, allowing anger to flow through her and making no effort to check her rising temper. How dared he keep teasing her—tormenting her in this uncaring way?

'Who I marry, when I marry, *if* I marry is my business, Dominic, not yours, so I suggest we drop the subject.' She could feel the fiery colour of embarrassment and anger tinging her cheeks and realised that her breathing was faster and shallower than it had been. Dominic always had the power, it seemed, to quicken her emotions into instant life.

Looking pleased by her reaction, Dominic's smile turned to one of complacency. 'Since you won't tell me about Robert,' he informed her slowly, 'I'll have to find out for myself! Let me take you both to dinner— tomorrow night, I think—then I can see for myself what your taste in men runs to.'

'No!'

Dominic's brow rose almost to disappear into his hair-line at her outburst as he looked even more amused, a smile tugging at the corners of his mobile mouth. '"No", Beth?'

'Er. . .I mean. . . No, thank you. I couldn't. . .er. . .that is. . .we couldn't. . .'

'Nonsense, Beth. I insist. Tomorrow night. Shall we say eight o'clock at—' he stopped and looked away from Beth for a moment, his eyes focused somewhere away in the distance, before switching back to her with sudden decisiveness '—the Trattoria. We enjoyed our last meal there, didn't we?' His smile looked more forced this time but relaxed again as he added, moving away from her to his own office, 'I'll book the table. You just turn up with Robert, looking gorgeous.' He stopped and turned back to her again, grinning openly. 'You looking gorgeous, of course, not Robert.'

By lunchtime the next day Beth was decidedly on edge. Dominic had been looking smug ever since he had arrived at work that morning when he had asked, 'All set for tonight, Beth?'

It had taken her all night to perfect her plan and, although she wasn't overly happy with what she had come up with, she thought it would work. And it had the advantage over the other ideas she had concocted of being simple. Fairly simple. There was little to go wrong.

Without going too deeply into her motives, she had abandoned any idea of telling Dominic the truth. Nor had it taken her long to realise that telling Dominic that that evening wasn't convenient to Robert wouldn't help either. He would only arrange another day. The only way round it was to apparently go along with the plan and then abort it at the last minute. She crossed her fingers and hoped that it would work.

Right on time the telephone rang at four fifty-five, and Beth almost snatched the receiver from its cradle. Dominic, who by luck rather than planning was in her office, gave her a quick glance of surprise at the hasty movement, but didn't say anything.

'OK, Beth, I'm phoning. Now what?' Cassie's conspiratorial whisper sounded unnaturally loud in Beth's ears and she glanced anxiously at Dominic, praying that he couldn't hear anything—not least that the caller was a woman.

'Robert. Is anything the matter?' Beth hoped she sounded convincing, not only about who she was talking to but surprised at the call—rather than something she had set up with Cassie early that morning.

'Are you sure this is going to work?' Cassie's tone suggested that she was less than convinced.

'What do you mean, you're held up? Where? Why?' Unsure whether she should sound concerned or irritated, Beth succeeded only in sounding wooden. Fortunately she didn't see the grin Dominic barely suppressed at her words.

The rest of her conversation consisted of 'Yes', 'No', 'I see', an 'Of course' and a final 'I'll tell him', while Cassie developed a fit of the giggles at the other end of the line.

She managed to suppress her chuckles long enough to say, 'Phone me later to tell me how he takes it,' before she hung up.

By the time Beth lifted her eyes to confront Dominic he had gained control of his features and was giving a creditable performance of someone mildly interested in half of someone else's phone conversation.

'Not bad news from Robert, I hope?' he asked smoothly, causing Beth's heart to lurch and skip a beat as she wondered uneasily whether he had heard anything he shouldn't.

'Yes, I'm afraid it is.' She lowered her eyes as she spoke, unable to meet his and tell an outright lie.

'Afraid, Beth?' he queried, the corners of his mouth twitching as he ruthlessly controlled a smile. 'Why afraid?'

That, at least, caused her to meet his gaze head-on. 'A figure of speech,' she pointed out tartly, before plunging into her fabricated tale. 'Robert is held up at a meeting— miles away. He says he'll be there another couple of hours at least and doesn't see how he can possibly make it back in time. I'm afraid. . .sorry. . .that we'll have to forgo having dinner with you tonight. But thank you for the invitation.' Beth ran through her rehearsed speech rather too fast but with no tripping over her words, she noted with satisfaction.

'What a shame,' Dominic told her, straight-faced, noticing with an inward grin that Beth almost sagged with relief. If he had ever wondered if she had lied to him in the past her current poor showing would have convinced him that she hadn't. The inward smile became physically manifest as he continued, 'I don't see why

that should stop us enjoying ourselves, though. *We* can
still have dinner.'

'What?' Beth couldn't—*wouldn't*—believe she had
heard aright. Dominic just *had* to be teasing.

'Marianne's looking forward to meeting you again,'
he went on as though she hadn't spoken, and since her
voice had been a strangled squeak he could be forgiven
for not hearing it.

Up until that moment Beth hadn't believed that things
could get worse, but as she heard to Dominic's words
she felt her spirits plummet even further. How could she
possibly sit opposite Marianne all evening, making polite
conversation and maintaining a cheerful, unconcerned
face, when she would be dying slowly inside? There was
a quality in Dominic's voice when he spoke of Marianne
which had been absent with previous girlfriends. It was
a tone which conveyed to Beth's tortured imagination a
very special feeling, and she feared that this was the
woman Dominic was going to marry.

That she had liked Marianne seemed to make matters
worse rather than better. It should be enough for her that
Dominic was going to be happy, but it made her feel
guilty about self-indulgent daydreams in which Marianne
mysteriously disappeared for ever and Beth could take
her place. Had the other woman been more in the Helena
Graham mould, she could have convinced herself that
Dominic would never have been happy with her. It would
almost have been her duty to protect Dominic from her.
As it was, her guilty fantasies only made her unhappiness
sharper.

Desperately trying to focus on what Dominic was saying to her, Beth managed to indicate that she didn't want
picking up and that she would make her own way to the
restaurant.

'Take a taxi,' Dominic advised, 'otherwise you won't
be able to drink anything.'

Beth had been planning to use her car, both for the excuse it gave her not to drink—for she was sure she was going to need all her wits about her—and so that she wouldn't get trapped into a lift home from Dominic. She heaved a sigh of resignation and gave in to the inevitable.

The evening was going to be unmitigated hell but somehow she would get through it. Tommorrow she would hand in her notice. She could not go on like this, living a day-to-day existence and hoping that something would happen to make her dreams come true. That had been going on too long.

It was time, finally, for the butterfly to emerge from the chrysalis and spread her wings, leaving her previous stages behind her as another, separate life. A butterfly only lives for twenty-four hours, she remembered, then its moment of glory was over. Even so, she had a sneaking suspicion that a butterfly would make more long-term plans than she had done. That was something she was going to change. Starting tomorrow.

Dominic's hands lingered a moment on her shoulders as he helped Beth on with her coat, and a frisson of awareness shot through her. Much as she wanted to relax and sink backwards into those waiting arms, she couldn't.

The evening had gone better than Beth had hoped, and if she could only get through the next five minutes it would all be over. Marianne had been determined to put Beth at her ease and had skilfully taken the conversation into her own hands at the beginning of the evening, exercising a subtle control over the other two ever since. It had been light-hearted, easy, fun—nothing too personal and probing and nothing Beth couldn't handle.

One or two pointed remarks from Dominic early on had either been diverted or ignored by Marianne, and if he had been planning to needle Beth he had given up the idea with good grace and a wry twist of the lips.

Marianne and Dominic obviously had a relationship which went back many years, leaving Beth to wonder idly if the two families were friends. That would explain the easy, teasing quality of the relationship, but it did nothing to remove the conviction that this was the woman Dominic intended to marry.

'We'll all go back to my flat for coffee.' Marianne fixed Dominic with a steely look, as though daring him to defy her, but he merely shrugged his broad shoulders and nodded acceptance.

Stammering out what she hoped was a polite refusal, Beth couldn't make out what she felt about the sudden invitation. Surely he would want some time alone with Marianne? He couldn't want her intruding. Come to that, why did the other girl want her there? Her expression had hinted at something more than mere politeness. One look at Marianne's face told Beth that any objections or excuses she raised would be summarily dealt with.

She gave in to the inevitable and found herself sitting in the front of the car beside Dominic with Marianne ensconced in the back, stifling a yawn but still insisting that the other two must have coffee.

'I want you to see my hall with the lamp,' she informed Beth, 'and judge for yourself.' A grunt from Dominic brought forth a chuckle of amusement. 'Dominic doesn't like it,' she explained to Beth, apparently unconcerned by this, adding, 'He can be terribly reactionary and con-servative at times. Can't you?' The latter question was accompanied by another soft laugh, but a conciliatory hand was laid on his shoulder in a gentle squeeze, taking the sting out of the words.

'I thought it was fine as it was,' was his only comment, but Beth saw him glance in the driving mirror and smile, his eyes meeting Marianne's. It seemed he wasn't too put out by her comments. That in itself testified to the depth and strength of their relationship, Beth thought glumly.

'He can be a real stick-in-the-mud,' Marianne continued. 'He hates change.'

'That's not strictly true.' Dominic clearly felt compelled to intervene in his own defence, but didn't sound seriously concerned by Marianne's description of him. 'Although some things are better left alone. Not all change is an improvement.'

She couldn't be sure but Beth had the strange sensation that Dominic shot her a sideways glance as he said that. Did he really mean that he wished she had stayed as she was, that she hadn't changed?

The hall was dramatic, exotic, and suited Marianne admirably. The lampshade looked entirely right. Beth couldn't help contrasting the deep, vivid colour, the sheen of the walls and the variety of textures with her own subtle greys, which suddenly seemed dull, insipid and boring rather than sophisticated.

Left alone with Dominic while Marianne bustled away to make coffee, Beth was strangely tongue-tied. There was so much she wanted to say, and none of it possible.

'Do you *really* like it?' Dominic broke the silence, his voice oddly stilted, leading Beth to look at him with incomprehension. 'The hall,' he tacked on when she didn't reply.

'Oh. . .er. . .yes,' she stumbled, and then tried to sound more positive. 'It's very imaginative. . .and it suits her.'

'I prefer yours,' he told her with quiet sincerity. 'It's subtle and restful and it suits you.' He stopped, as though unsure whether to continue, but then went on, 'I could live with your hall. . .but not with what Marianne has out there. I could—' He broke off, coughed and turned to face Beth as he spoke the last words, his eyes meeting and holding hers—the expression in them causing her heart to quicken its beating as blood pounded in her temples.

'Beth. . .' Whatever he had been going to say was lost in the clatter of cups and saucers as Marianne pushed her way into the room, carrying a precariously balanced tray.

What had he been going to say? Beth didn't understand Dominic and just wanted to be gone. She couldn't believe that his words meant what they seemed to imply. And if they did, what was he doing telling her—and in Marianne's flat of all places? She drank her coffee as quickly as she decently could, scalding her tongue in the process, so anxious was she to be gone.

'Would you mind if I phoned for a taxi?' she asked Marianne, and wondered at the look of surprise in the other girl's eyes which was quickly replaced by amusement.

'No!'

'Nonsense. Dominic will take you home.' They spoke together and Beth wondered whether she had really heard the 'No' spring so readily to Dominic's lips.

'I couldn't put him to all that bother.' Beth addressed her remark to Marianne but it was Dominic who replied.

'It's no bother.' With that he was on his feet, and Beth had no option but to get up, too. To say anything else now would be to make too great an issue out of it and she didn't want them to think that she was trying to avoid being alone with him. Either one of them might start putting two and two together—and coming up with the right answer!

CHAPTER EIGHT

'WERE you only being polite to Marianne about the hall?' Dominic asked, sounding as though he couldn't quite believe she had been telling the truth earlier. 'It doesn't seem to be your style. Too flamboyant. Not you at all!'

Beth's head swung round sharply to look at him but Dominic kept his eyes fixed firmly on the road ahead, presenting her with a dazzling view of his imposing profile.

'I'm not sure how to take that,' she informed him with hauteur, and was rewarded by Dominic taking his eyes from the road to flash a quick, almost conspiritorial grin at her.

'Which bit—about being polite or about being flamboyant?' He didn't give her time to answer as he went on, 'For all the changes you've made to yourself, Beth, I would never describe you as flamboyant!'

Silently Beth gritted her teeth. Already she was beginning to hate the word—the more often Dominic used it the odder it sounded. Flam-boy-ant.

'You may now be superficially more sophisticated and glamorous, but underneath the make-up and new clothes I can't help thinking that the old Beth is still there and would be very happy to resurface.'

As she listened to this high-handed, pompous and supremely arrogant speech Beth's mouth dropped open, forming a perfectly shaped O. Surely she must be hallucinating, she thought, grasping at straws. Dominic couldn't really mean what he was saying. Focusing on the road stretching out ahead as she struggled to believe that what her ears were telling her was true, she heard Dominic's voice adding, 'Come on Beth, admit that it's true. Keeping up this new image is more effort than it's worth. Let's go back to how things were.'

The strangled sound which escaped Beth's lips was one of total disbelief as she ransacked her brain for something sensible to say—but nothing occurred to her. How could she possibly say anything sensible to such outrageousness?

'No comment, Beth?' Dominic's quietly drawled words caused her to swing back to look at him. She found him grinning wickedly, although his attention was still fixed on his driving. 'You can shut your mouth now,' he told her, feigning concern. 'To look *so* shocked doesn't do much for your fabled cope-with-anything image.'

'You were teasing!' As quickly as her fury dissipated when she realised that he hadn't meant a word of what he had said there came a new, hurting anger. Anger that he should, could, tease her in that way. The changes she had made—not just in how she looked, but how she behaved and how she approached life—were very precious to her and that he should see fit to belittle them told her how little he really thought of her. What he had said went far beyond any normal definition of the word teasing. He couldn't care for her at all.

'It took you long enough to work that out! I was wondering how far I would have to go.' Dominic's tone changed from amused laughter to a more thoughtful tone, a frown creasing his brow as an unpleasant thought struck him. 'You couldn't possibly have thought I meant it!'

When Beth remained stubbornly silent his voice vibrated with horror and his frown became even fiercer. 'Beth, you did! How could you?'

The car drew to a smooth halt outside her flat and, swiftly unfastening the seat belt and gathering up her bag, Beth prepared to make a quick departure without

saying another word. In that she was thwarted by
Dominic who grabbed hold of her arm, pulling her back
so that she was forced to face him. Pleased to see that
he now looked thoroughly rattled, Beth stood, or rather
sat, her ground. It looked as though stony silence might
be the best policy.

'Tell me you're teasing me now,' he almost demanded.
'You deserve to get your own back. You *couldn't* have
believed I meant it.'

With quiet dignity Beth brought her eyes up to meet
his. Although much of her anger had been replaced with
wicked delight at his discomfiture, she saw no reason to
help him out. He had upset her—let him have a taste of
his own medicine. After what he had said he deserved
to suffer.

'Is it so surprising I believed you?' she asked him
softly, shaking her head with a slow, almost sad motion
as she dipped her head to hide her face, not at all sure
she could control the grin of triumph which threatened
to break through and give the game away. 'You have
so often seemed to resent the changes I've made. You
seem. . .'

Aware that she was beginning to sound emotional,
Beth took a steadying breath. She was telling him very
much more than she had intended. 'You say you were
teasing, Dominic, but I wonder if that's really true? I
think you meant more of what you said than you're
prepared to admit, even to yourself.'

The shocked expression on Dominic's face told Beth
that he could barely take in what she was saying. The
frown returned and he looked as though he was getting
ready to deny what she had said.

'Think about it, Dominic,' she told him, watching as
his eyes darkened until they appeared almost black.

With her parting words leaving Dominic totally
stunned, Beth was out of the car and into her building

before he could react. As she ran up the stairs, fighting
back hot, stupid tears—her high heels clattering on the
stone steps—she heard a sound behind her. The sound
of a man running, heavy footfalls on the stone steps. It
was enough to spur her on. It could only be Dominic
chasing after her and she simply wasn't able to cope with
him just then. What she needed was to be alone to deal
with her feelings—to face up to how little Dominic took
her changes seriously and how little he cared for her and
her feelings to tease her as he had.

She gained the top-floor landing, her breath coming
in deep, rasping gasps as she fought back the tears and
fumbled with fingers which seemed to have become all
thumbs as she struggled to unlock her door and gain
sanctuary. She very nearly made it.

As she felt the lock turn Dominic's lean, brown hand
shot past her shoulder to force the door wide open before
he pushed her into the hall, slamming the door behind
him in the same, swift movement.

'Go away, Dominic.' Beth forced the words past the
lump in her throat, striving to sound normal.

'You can't say such things and just walk away!'
Dominic was beginning to sound more angry than confused and that was enough to fire Beth's temper again.
If he had sounded apologetic, hurt even, she wouldn't
have been able to withstand him. But anger she could
stand up to. What right had he to be angry?

'*I* can't say such things?' she demanded, inwardly
screaming the words and surprised to hear how in control
she sounded. '*I* can say what I like, Dominic, when we're
not at work, and particularly now in my own house. And
what I'm saying is that I want you to leave. Now!'

'No.' Dominic's eyes had been fixed on her face as
she had been speaking and something he saw there must
have made him see things differently as some of the
anger dropped from his voice. When he spoke his voice

was quieter. 'No, Beth. We're going to talk this out. Now!'

'If you don't leave this instant I'm going to call the police.' Mistake, Beth, she realised as she heard herself make the threat. What did she know about assertiveness? Never make threats unless you intend to carry them through.

She knew she wasn't going to call the police and, judging by the grin on Dominic's face, he knew it too. That one, silly phrase had lost her her position and rocked her confidence. The only way she could see now of trying to regain lost ground was to go along with what he wanted but refuse to be swayed by anything he said.

The curving arch of his raised brow told Beth that Dominic knew she had overplayed her hand and she didn't need to see the smile that twisted his lips to realise that he would take full advantage of the situation. She expected him to dare her to call the police, to call her bluff, but he surprised her by ignoring the impetuous statement. It was demoralising to realise that he knew he didn't have to bother to make his point. The advantage was already his.

'Why don't you make us some coffee?' Dominic suggested, moving towards the living room. A painful sensation of *déjà vu* came over Beth as her mind replayed the last time he had visited her flat.

'You won't be staying that long,' she told him, unable to trust herself to pretend that things were normal between them. When were things ever normal these days?

Not since the emergence of the new Beth, she reminded herself, and accepted that she couldn't lay all the blame at Dominic's door. She had demanded that he adapted to her—made changes in his own life—without ever considering what impact these changes might have had. Without ever asking whether he'd wanted to make them. She was entitled to change, to want things to be different, but she had never really considered whether Dominic had had the right to expect everything to stay the way it had been.

Cassie had tried to explain some of this to her, but she hadn't listened. She hadn't *wanted* to listen. Maybe Dominic was right and they did have things to discuss. In fact, put like that, maybe this talk was long overdue.

As Beth's essential fairness led her to think more kindly of Dominic, part of her was trying to scream a warning. Be careful, he'll take advantage. You *let* him take advantage. You're too soft-hearted, too prone to seeing the other person's point of view. It's ingrained in you. You still haven't learnt that sometimes you *do* have the right to be selfish, to want things for yourself, to stand up for your own rights.

'No coffee, no mercy—is that the strategy, Bethesda?' Dominic's taunt was just what she needed to strengthen her resolve and, without giving him another glance, she swept ahead of him into the living room—assuming that he would follow.

'What is it you want to say?' She swung round to face him, intending to catch him off guard—only to be thrown into confusion herself as she almost collided with him. He had closed in on her without her noticing and now they were only inches apart.

'Careful, Beth.' He caught her by the arms and steadied her as one high heel caught in the carpet, turning her ankle over so that she almost fell. 'You haven't had too much to drink, have you?' he asked mock-solicitously, since they both knew exactly how much, or how little, she had drunk. 'You'd better sit down.'

With that, Dominic steered her towards the sofa, and before she could do otherwise Beth found herself sitting at one end of the sofa with Dominic next to her, having been outmanoeuvred by a master.

She had had no intention of sitting anywhere near him

and she was certain he knew that. Why else was he grinning at her in that particularly devilish way he had? That particular grin was not unknown to Beth, who had seen it before and recognised it as the one he displayed when he thought he had brought off a particularly difficult and delicate negotiation.

As he continued to watch her the grin faded from Dominic's face, and the amusement which had been evident in his eyes disappeared until all that was left was seriousness and something which could have been concern.

'No games, Beth,' he told her as her troubled grey eyes met his unflinchingly. 'I think the time has come for us to be totally honest with each other and to find out where we're going. What do you say?'

She couldn't find the words to say anything, and left Dominic to interpret the slight movement of her head as a nod of agreement. With a fateful sense of inevitability, Beth admitted that he was right—they couldn't go on acting as they had been. There were a number of issues to be resolved, and now was as good a time as any.

For a moment neither of them said anything, just continued to look at the other. Beth wondered if the memory of the last time they had shared the sofa came to them at the same moment. In the instant she felt colour spreading into her cheeks Dominic suddenly drew back from her to sit slightly further away from her, his arm along the back of the sofa. Near her, but in no danger of touching her.

'Maybe I will make coffee.' The excuse for action sprang unbidden to her lips but Dominic caught her hand as she went to move.

'It's too late for that, Beth. You can't keep running.'

And suddenly there was no space between them as he drew her down again so that she half fell onto the sofa, more of her in contact with Dominic than she had expected or wanted. But even as she was telling herself that she had to get away from him her body was responding in its own way to press closer to him. And Dominic didn't seem to mind. Rather than pushing her away, his hands were gathering her to him, his arms going round her as his mouth came towards hers.

Beth was still inwardly fighting him right up to the moment his lips touched hers. At the first, tentative meeting she gave up her inner battle with herself and was lost.

Why not? she wondered. It's what I want, and I need something of Dominic to remember. It was as though the decision had been taken from her—or she had finally acknowledged a decision she had made some time ago. She would have to leave Dominic. She couldn't possibly go on working with him, knowing how little real respect he had for her. But she would have these memories to take with her.

Dearly held beliefs vanished as, meeting no resistance, the pressure of Dominic's mouth on hers increased as he deepened the kiss. How can you let him do this, part of her mind asked, when you know he has no regard for you? I don't care, another part responded. This is what I want.

Her arms wound themselves round his shoulders, pulling him closer to her, and in response Dominic pushed her back against the soft cushions of the sofa. His hands were hard against her shoulders before his grip slackened and he loosened his hold to let them slip slowly downwards until each hand cupped one full breast, his thumbs running slowly, tantalisingly, across their peaks until Beth felt her whole body fill with a deep, throbbing awareness of a desire she had never felt before.

Her body squirmed against Dominic's in response and anticipation as his head came down to hers once more and their lips met. This time his tongue pushed insistently against her teeth and forced her mouth to open, giving him access to the warm, wet cavern, his tongue meeting and twining with hers.

The sensations that ripped through her were so intense that she didn't notice that his hands were leaving her body to reach for the zip of her dress until he was lifting her up off the couch to push it off her shoulders. Even as she was protesting, her arms came free of the sleeves and she felt cool air caressing her heated skin as Dominic let his eyes drop to feast on her breasts, half-concealed by the lace and satin of her flimsy bra.

Stop this now, the old, cautious Beth was telling her, while the newer, more adventurous Beth was saying, Go with it, enjoy it. The decision was made for her and with one quick, neat movement—obviously, Beth thought, the result of much practice—Dominic had removed her bra, along with her dress, and dropped them on the floor.

No amount of new positive thinking could stop the hot colour flooding her body as embarrassment swamped her and she tried vainly to cover herself with hands which were inadequate to the task. A throaty chuckle escaped from somewhere deep in Dominic's chest at her gesture as he caught her hands in his own, pulling them away from her body to hold them at her sides as he looked his fill at her.

'Don't be embarrassed, Beth,' he told her. 'I've wanted to see you like this for so long. You wouldn't disappoint me now, would you?' The desire that filled his eyes, causing them to glitter in the low light, held Beth in its spell and some of the anxiety left her as Dominic's head dipped once more to her, caressingly leaving a trail of points of fire from the kisses he pressed on her as he made his way in a slow zigzag down and across her body from neck to shoulders until he finally reached her waiting breasts.

Beth relaxed in his hold, her hands still pinned to her sides as Dominic used his mouth to arouse her beyond anything she had ever known. The throbbing inside her was becoming more insistent, more urgent, and Beth couldn't repress another wriggle, only to find as she did so that Dominic moved so that he was lying on top of her, the hard contours of his body pressing against her as his weight pushed her deeper into the softness of the sofa.

The deep moan that left her throat, half forcing itself into his name, acted like a release to his restraint and suddenly her hands were as free to explore him as Dominic's were roaming over her. She was pushing his shirt away from his shoulders before she was even aware of having undone the buttons, revelling in the feel of the crisp hairs on his chest as they rasped against her soft skin.

She slipped one hand between them to twine her fingers in the downy hair while she pressed frantic kisses into his neck and along his shoulder. Her body arched against his as she felt desire flaring through her, and her teeth raked Dominic's skin as she gave herself up to the unfamiliar sensations.

There was a deep moan of satisfaction from Dominic as, holding her tightly to him, he rolled over onto his back and pulled Beth over with him so that she was lying on top of him, her legs slipping and sliding until they came to rest on either side of his body in an effort not to fall from her precariously balanced position on the sofa.

Dominic was holding her wrists again, keeping her in position as he said, 'There's no need to rush, Beth, is there? We've got all night. Much as I want you now, this minute, I think we'll both be more comfortable if we give up on the sofa and go and find your bed.'

His words, despite being interspersed with numerous kisses to all the parts of her that his mouth could reach, nevertheless acted like a bucket of cold water over Beth. One minute she had been alive, hot with desire for him, wanting only to please him and have him please her. The next she was bumping down to earth with an overwhelming sense of shame and embarrassment as the magic balloon of make-believe deflated into cold reality.

Dominic didn't care for her—hadn't he proved that already tonight? True, he might want her, and Beth's intimate contact with his body told her that he wasn't lying about that, but wanting wasn't the same as caring, respecting, loving. Dully Beth admitted to herself that although she cared for Dominic, that she even loved him, somewhere along the line she had ceased to respect him. Much as part of her wanted to continue the erotic game they were playing, wanted to give herself to Dominic, she knew that she couldn't. She wanted to make love with Dominic, but what they were doing didn't feature love. He didn't love her. He loved. . .

How could she have forgotten! Marianne. She pushed herself away from him and made an undignified scramble to her feet, not caring that one carelessly moved knee jabbed Dominic in the stomach or that a trailing foot landed another blow. Dominic grunted in pain and surprise, struggling to push himself onto one elbow to regard her with astonishment.

'Beth? What on earth's the matter?' If she hadn't known him better she would have sworn that there was hurt as well as disappointment in his voice.

Struggling into her dress with her back to him, Beth surreptitiously kicked her discarded bra under the sofa—not wanting to prolong the sense of intimacy by putting it on in front of Dominic or wanting it in sight as silent testimony to what they had shared.

'I've come to my senses, that's all,' she answered him, sliding the zip up as far as she could reach without an ungainly struggle and turning to face him.

It was nearly her downfall. Dominic was still sprawled along the sofa, leaning on one elbow, his naked torso with its light covering of dark hair disturbingly masculine. She remembered how smooth his skin had felt under her enquiring fingers, the overlay of firm muscle covering bone and the supple strength evident with every move he had made as his hands and body had explored hers.

The confusion in his eyes as they met hers looked so genuine that for a second she faltered. . . Was she wrong. . .? He obviously wanted her. . .

But common sense reasserted itself. He might want her now, but what did that prove? Just that he was a normal, healthy, red-blooded male and that he found her at least passably attractive. She didn't even try to control the distaste she was feeling from showing in her face. Disgust with him, but particularly with herself for getting carried away by physical longings to the exclusion of all else. As her emotions played across her features the look she bestowed on Dominic couldn't be misinterpreted.

The confusion in his eyes was slowly giving way to something more negative and he swung his legs to the ground, getting to his feet to come and stand before her.

He made no effort to dress and the nearness of his naked chest was causing Beth's breathing to become shallow and more rapid as the arousing male smell of him reached her once more. Clenching her hands into fists, she willed herself not to make a move towards him, not to reach out to run a finger along the ridge of muscle or push fingers through the hair on his chest until she reached his shoulders and could pull him to her.

The air vibrated with the tension between them, and just when Beth thought she could stand it no longer and would have to touch Dominic and give in to the craving which was tearing her mind and body apart Dominic himself broke the spell.

He picked up his shirt from where she had discarded it and slowly thrust one arm into a sleeve, dragging it round behind his back as his other arm searched for the second sleeve. It was like watching a striptease in reverse, and nearly as exciting. Unable to wrench her eyes away from the play of his muscles, Beth simply watched him. An act which did not go unnoticed by Dominic.

'What's the matter now, Beth? Regretting your hasty decision? Unfortunately, I think you're too late for a change of mind. I've decided that I don't want to make love to you after all. I thought you had changed, that you had grown up enough to handle real emotions—to be able to handle a real man—but it seems I was wrong.

'You still want to run away and hide, don't you? To pretend that people don't have feelings, don't have needs. You're as frightened of men, of sex, as you ever were. Well, you needn't worry about having to fight me off ever again. I've learnt my lesson tonight. I'm too old to play these sorts of games with frigid little girls who don't want to grow up. We could have had so much together, Beth, but you're too frightened to try.'

Still Beth's eyes followed him as he roughly pushed his shirt into the waistband of his trousers. She heard his words, listened to what he said, but she resisted, both intellectually and emotionally, understanding what they meant. She knew that her composure wouldn't hold out if she really took in what Dominic was telling her. And that was because she knew that she would have to question whether he was right, and that she didn't want to do.

Some time in the early hours of the morning when she had no more tears left to shed Beth acknowledged the truth of much of what Dominic had said. She *was* frightened of admitting her feelings, and the feelings of others, but not as much as she had been. It wasn't so much that she had a problem but that she had had no practice.

A quiet, shy girl, what she had told Dominic was true. She had taken refuge in work and never really learnt how to handle romantic relationships. Given more time, and

some support and understanding, she thought that she
could overcome the inhibitions that remained.

But Dominic hadn't wanted that. He was impatient.
He wasn't prepared to go slowly enough for her to feel
comfortable, to feel safe—not only with his needs and
feelings, but with hers. And there was the unanswered
question that was Marianne and his relationship with her.

It was one thing to accept her love for Dominic in the
secrecy of her heart, to hug it to her like a comforter,
but quite another to admit that loving Dominic meant
accepting all kinds of needs and desires. And if Dominic
cared for her at all then denying the existence of such
needs was even more difficult. Facing him at work was
going to be hard and, it seemed to Beth, something she
couldn't keep on doing.

Sooner or later they would find themselves in the same
situation again; indeed, Dominic might even go out of
his way to engineer it—despite his protestations to the
contrary—and she wasn't sure that she could continue
to withstand the pressure of her feelings and the demands
of Dominic's body and her own.

This was crunch time. No longer could she bury her
head in the sand like some frightened ostrich—she had
to face up to the inevitable. And that meant leaving
Dominic and finding another job.

The only other option she could see was to have an
affair with Dominic, if that was what he was really
angling for, and Beth felt unequal to coping with that.
She would only end up even more hurt and still have to
leave her job. Better to go now. It might be a coward's
way out, but Beth wasn't pretending otherwise. Better a
safe coward, she told herself, than a sorry. . .and stead-
fastly refused to fill in what she might be comparing
herself to.

*   *   *

Coming slowly awake, Beth glanced at the clock and then looked more carefully. With a stifled groan she hurried towards the bathroom. It would have to be *this* morning that she overslept, wouldn't it?

It was twenty past nine as she put her coat on, preparatory to leaving, when the phone rang.

'Where the hell are you?'

No hello, no social pleasantries, Beth noticed grimly, just a very angry male making demands.

'Obviously I'm at home,' she answered sweetly, surprised that Dominic's anger appeared to have banished most, if not all, of her anxiety. It only went to prove that he was not worth agonising over.

'Why aren't you here? What are you playing at, Bethesda?' Dominic still sounded very angry and Beth gnawed gently on her lower lip at his use of her name. Whenever he called her Bethesda she was aware of a silly weakness attacking her knees, causing them to develop a strange, rubbery consistency. How she wished she had never given in to the impulse to tell him her full name. And that's a lie, Bethesda Anderson, if ever there was one!

'I overslept.'

'What?'

'I overslept.' Her simple, straightforward admission seemed to dampen the fires of Dominic's anger and through the silence Beth could envisage him perched on the edge of his desk with the phone pressed against his ear, looking totally nonplussed. As several seconds passed and he still said nothing Beth felt more in control, both of herself and the situation. There was a certain numbness about her which made thinking largely irrelevant as she acted almost on autopilot.

'I was just putting my coat on. I'll be in shortly.'

'Right.'

'I'm sorry I'm late.'

'Fine.' Dominic's words sounded slightly odd, a vague strangled sound, as though he was having trouble getting them past some obstruction in his throat.

'Did you ring me for anything important?'

'What?' Why on earth should Dominic sound so startled by such a simple question? she wondered. He must have phoned her with some purpose in mind.

'Why did you phone? Was it important?'

'No. . .yes!' The struggle Dominic was having articulating seemed to be getting worse. 'That is, I thought maybe you weren't coming in at all.'

'Oh!'

'Yes. Oh!'

The buzzing in her ear told Beth that Dominic had hung up, and as she carefully replaced the reciever she wondered exactly what that last 'Yes. Oh!' had meant. Her attack of nerves came back with a vengeance.

CHAPTER NINE

ALL day Dominic treated Beth carefully, acting as if he were walking on egg shells and treating Beth as though she was recovering from some dread illness or as though she had had bad news. It was as if he was watching every word he said, and the longer it went on the more uneasy Beth felt.

No mention was made of the disastrous outcome of the night before, nor had either of them referred to his telephone call. His behaviour might be most uncharacteristic but Beth barely noticed, feeling too numb to even think about it.

The vague memory that she had planned to hand in her notice haunted her, but it required more co-ordinated action than she felt able to take. When no mention of Marianne was made she let the idea drift. She would have to leave some time, but the thought was so painful. She would find herself a good job first. Then it would look, and feel, less like running away.

She spent the next week away from the Commission, making visits to patients. Forcing herself to focus on them and their problems became easier as the days passed and Dominic receded to the back of her mind. She would have to think about the future soon, but not just yet. All the patients were doing well, getting appropriate treatment and back-up, and she took heart from that. To know that something was going right for someone, despite the patients' problems, began to restore her faith in the system being able to work.

Over coffee she reviewed the cases which were preying on her mind with Bob Muir.

'First Barry Miller. He's stabilised on medication and has been discharged on leave of absence again. A community nurse is in close contact with him, which will hopefully keep him taking his medication. His last outburst seems to have frightened him as much as everyone else and I think the memory of that will make him more compliant with medication, at least for a while.'

'So that's going well.'

'Yes. The hospital inquiry is under way. With our involvement and the statements from Barr and Gordon, there will be no whitewash. Andy McGregor will clearly lose his job.'

'What about McCann?'

Beth shrugged. 'I don't know. He deserves to go as well but. . .' She shrugged again. 'You know how these things are.'

'And what about Jenny Sullivan? That really got to you, didn't it?' Bob held up a hand. 'Don't deny it,' he told her when she would have protested.

'There wasn't any negligence. I can understand why Jenny's parents didn't want her to marry Bill. He is rough, uncouth and belligerent, but I don't think it was worse than that. A lot of the nurses' views about him came from the fact that Mr and Mrs Rankin were always saying how badly he treated Jenny.'

Bob patted her on the shoulder. 'Let it go,' he advised, 'and focus on the patients you're seeing now. Think about the future.'

The future, she thought bleakly. What of the future? She accepted that she had come to the end of her time with the Commission. It wasn't only her feelings for Dominic which were a problem. She missed clinical work—treating patients, staying with them and seeing them improve. She had enjoyed her work at the Commission enormously, had benefited from it and hoped that she had contributed to it, but now it was time to move on.

Dominic was only the final part of a decision she would have had to face sooner or later. She would put out some feelers for jobs and see what was about and what was coming up. There was a shortage of consultants and she didn't think it would take her long to get fixed up. Somehow it was easy not to think about Dominic. It was as though a steel shutter had come down in her mind, clanging shut and leaving him securely on the other side.

Beth knocked on the door again and waited. The previous patient hadn't been at home when she'd called and it looked as though Ewen Hunter was going to be another absentee. It was turning out to be one of those days. She tried one more time and was rewarded by thinking that she heard muffled sounds from inside the house. When nothing happened she decided that it must have been her imagination working overtime, based on wishful thinking.

She was just turning away when the door opened and was pulled back a fraction and a very dishevelled face appeared. Mr Hunter's hair was every which way and he had several days' growth of beard on his chin. To Beth's eyes it looked as though he had hurriedly donned trousers and shirt to answer the door for his feet were bare. She sighed. Ewen Hunter obviously wasn't doing very well.

'Who are you? What do you want?'

At his words Beth's opinion underwent a radical transformation. His voice was hoarse and husky and his breathing shallow and laboured. It didn't need the bout of coughing which followed the effort of speech to indicate that Mr Hunter's appearance had more to do with flu than his mental state. Having quickly explained who she was, Ewen Hunter seemed more than pleased to welcome her into his home.

'Forgot you were coming,' he explained. 'Sorry about the mess,' he muttered as he led her into his living room. 'Haven't felt like doing much for the last few days.'

'That sounds like a nasty chest, Mr Hunter,' Beth said, and got a wheezy grunt of what sounded like agreement in response.

'Bronchitis,' he confirmed.

'Have you seen your doctor?' Beth asked as the older man sank thankfully into an armchair.

'Saw some young lad at the surgery last week,' he confirmed. 'Not *my* doctor. Some locum. Seemed to think it was all in my imagination.' A fit of coughing overtook him. 'Didn't want to give me anything.' He took a ragged breath. 'Wanted to talk about my schizophrenia. I told him that was under control and that it was my chest, but he wouldn't listen. Kept asking me about voices.' His voice had risen resentfully as he spoke and ended in another bout of coughing as he managed to wheeze out, 'Never heard a voice in my life!'

Beth smiled to herself at the indignation in his tone but sobered quickly when she realised that it meant that he had not got the proper treatment he required because some young doctor had seen fit not to believe him. It was a problem a number of patients complained of. Once they were labelled psychotic everything was put down to that. As though someone who was psychotic couldn't be physically ill as well, Beth thought, now nearly as indignant as Mr Hunter.

'We'll see about that,' she promised. 'I think you need a home visit. Have you got your doctor's number?'

'Yes. . .' Ewen Hunter reached for a notebook on a side table '. . .but I haven't got a phone.'

'But I have,' said Beth with triumph, producing her mobile phone from her bag with a grin.

'Oh, very flash,' said a happier-looking Mr Hunter. 'And to think I've always been rude about people who saw the need to go around with their own phone!' He started to laugh but was again overtaken by a bout of coughing.

Having arranged for the GP to visit, Beth took her leave of him and said that she'd return in a week's time. To her practised eye it looked as though Ewen Hunter was doing well and could expect to be discharged, but she'd still like to see him when he was a bit fitter.

He saw her to the door. 'Goodbye, Doctor. And thanks for getting things fixed up. You psychiatrists have uses, after all.'

And if that isn't damning with faint praise I don't know what is, Beth thought, as she set off for her car and her next visit.

Beth had agreed to speak that evening at a local 'users' forum', the name given to a self-help group of current and ex-psychiatric patients who were involved in advocacy and empowerment. Their aim was very much to take control of their own lives and the management of their illnesses, and Beth was all for that. They often invited speakers along and Beth had heard from colleagues that they had received quite a grilling. Now it was her turn.

Having explained that the Commission in Scotland had wider powers than its sister organisation in England, she outlined these.

'You're still a psychiatrist, though, aren't you? Still one of them.' The stocky young man with the red hair and beard had gazed fixedly at Beth since she'd started speaking, leaving her to wonder just how long he would last before he interrupted her. He had gone longer than she had expected.

'Yes, it's true I'm a psychiatrist,' she agreed pleasantly, 'but I'd prefer not to think of an "us" and "them" senario. We need to try to work together and—'

'Rubbish! How can "we",' he sneered, '"work together" when you have the power to lock us up? You're supporting the system and—'

'No, she's not!' Another voice entered the argument.

As other voices were raised in support and dissent things were rapidly getting out of hand. The organiser didn't look as though she was going to do anything to bring order to the proceedings so Beth decided that it was up to her. Someone had to do something, and quickly, if things were not going to get totally out of control.

'Why don't you let me finish describing what *I* think we do,' she suggested loudly, raising her voice to carry over the hubbub, 'and then we can discuss what *you* think we do.'

Most people seemed to be happy with that since it had been the agreed plan anyway, although the red-headed man continued to glare at her.

Beth emphasised that their primary interest was in individuals receiving—or not receiving—a service, and pointed out that rather than always dealing with complaints about being badly treated most patients complained of not being seen often enough by a psychiatrist and of not being given enough of the services they wanted, particularly not enough—or not appropriate—daytime activities.

'We are a Royal Commission,' Beth ended, 'which means we are independent of Government. That, of course, is vital, if we are to maintain any kind of authority and independence to comment, criticise or act on the issues which we investigate.'

No sooner had she finished than her red-headed adversary launched into the attack, and for the next forty minutes Beth was fully engaged in both maintaining her side of the debate and stopping things from becoming too heated. Some of the comments between members were becoming unhelpfully personal and she was relieved when the organiser stepped in and declared the debate closed and the coffee ready.

Driving home, she told herself she was right to think about a clinical job. She was tired and it was time for a move.

'Beth! It's been a long time. How are you?' Jessica Balfour-Knight's bright tones rang across the enclosed confines of the shopping arcade and intruded into Beth's mental ramblings, although it was only when the other woman placed her bulk squarely in front of Beth that she really came to and noticed her surroundings. And her erstwhile colleague.

'Fine,' she responded automatically, taking in the changed appearance of the other woman. 'And, yes, it must be ages. You didn't look anything like that last time I saw you!'

'No.' Jessica gave her bulge an affectionate pat. 'I've still got two months to go. Do you think I can get bigger?' Her voice was rueful but her eyes twinkled, and Beth gave the answer she knew Jessica didn't want.

'Oh, yes. Heaps.' She grinned unrepentantly. 'I remember when I was a student a woman who—'

'I'd really rather you didn't,' Jessica informed her mock-sorrowfully, accepting that she wasn't going to get any sympathy. 'Keep your reminiscences to yourself, please. Anyway, I'd rather hear about what's caused the change in *your* appearance.'

It was Beth's turn to look rueful. 'Nothing as exciting as a baby,' she murmured, not realising how wistful she sounded, but her tone caused Jessica to eye her thoughtfully.

'Let's have lunch and catch up.'

Seated at a window table overlooking the Italian Centre, Jessica gave Beth another shrewdly appraising glance. 'You look fantastic. I'd heard there'd been a

change of image.' She gave an apologetic shrug. 'You
know how everyone gossips, and the men are the worst!'
A slight frown creased her brow. 'In fact, I think it was
Michael who mentioned it first.'

'Yes. . .well. . . It was time for a change.' Beth felt
uncomfortable discussing her appearance. She knew that
it was irrational to assume that no one had noticed, or
commented, or speculated, but she hated to think of the
conclusions they had drawn.

'And where does the devastating Dominic fit in?'
Jessica was nothing if not straightforward, and saw no
reason for beating about the bush.

'Dominic? Nowhere.' Even as she uttered the lie Beth
could feel a wave of colour staining her cheeks and
proclaiming the falsehood for what it was. Fortunately
Jessica didn't appear to notice.

'You know, I think I made a mistake in marrying
Michael.' Beth's colour receded and she gaped open-
mouthed at Jessica. She had always thought that the
Knights were idyllically happy. 'All those gorgeous men
out there, lost to me for ever.' Jessica sighed theatrically
and Beth let out a breath of relief, recognising when she
was being teased.

'And you're married to one of the most gorgeous,'
Beth told her firmly, remembering the blond giant Jessica
had married. Hunk was the only word.

'Yes,' Jessica agreed smugly, 'but Dominic is *nearly*
as gorgeous.'

'But. . .' Realising that she was about to suggest that
Dominic was better-looking in the tall, dark, chiselled
mould than a blond Viking warrior, Beth bit back the
words. Not only would it be bad-mannered, it would
open up an area for discussion that she would prefer
to ignore. Like her partiality for tall, dark, handsome
psychiatrists called Dominic. Wanting to change the sub-

ject, she said the first thing that came into her head. 'I'm looking for a new job.'

'Really?' Jessica sounded surprised at first, but then her brows narrowed and she nodded to herself as though confirming some inner thought. 'Probably a good idea. You've been at the Commission a while now.'

It was Beth's turn to be surprised. Somehow she had expected people to try to talk her out of it. Maybe she really was more due for a change than she had realised. 'I've not mentioned it to. . .' She trailed away again, not wanting to put ideas into Jessica's mind, but the other woman didn't seem to think there was anything odd in that.

'No, of course not.' She paused for a moment, then added, 'You know they're about to advertise two consultant posts in the south sector, don't you?'

'I didn't think it was going to be so soon.' Everyone knew that the posts were coming up so Jessica wasn't giving away too much.

'Michael was telling me the other day. Both community posts. Suit you down to the ground.'

'Yes.' It was exactly what she wanted—in an area where a lot of new, exciting things were happening—so why didn't she feel more enthusiastic? She wouldn't think about not seeing Dominic, she told herself, she simply wouldn't.

'I'll tell Michael you're interested, shall I?' Jessica asked, and it took all Beth's will-power to nod.

Despite her decision not to ask advice, Sunday found her discussing Dominic and her prospective job change with Cassie who, to Beth's astonishment, was totally against it.

'How can I possibly discuss it with Dominic?' Beth demanded of her friend over what she saw as a particularly naïve suggestion.

'At least tell him you're thinking of moving,' Cassie

implored. 'Give Dominic the chance to tell you what he *really* thinks. All this second-guessing isn't getting either of you anywhere.'

'Suppose he says he wants me to leave?' Beth's clear grey eyes clouded over at the disturbing thought. It was one thing to envision leaving but quite another to know that Dominic would be glad to see her go.

'If nothing else, you'll know exactly where you stand,' Cassie pointed out pragmatically. 'I can't help but feel that if you leave you'll regret it, and will keep wondering what might have happened if you'd stayed. That's no basis to build a secure future on.'

And that, Beth reflected, got to the heart of the situation. No matter how much she *thought* that the sensible thing to do was to leave—to make a clean break before the heartache got worse—listening to the voice of reason was hard. Her mind said go, her heart said stay. While she stayed there was always hope, but if she left—if she left, Dominic would have forgotten her in a matter of days.

The real issue, she knew, was how much she was prepared to risk getting hurt—to find out what Dominic really thought and felt. And to admit openly what she felt.

'Maybe you're right,' she conceded, and gave a half-hearted smile when Cassie nodded vigorously.

'Of course I am! And if George was here I'm sure he'd agree with me.' She sounded so determined that Beth's smile widened.

'He wouldn't dare do anything else,' she confirmed, and in response to the telling glance bestowed on her by Cassie she hastened to ask after her friend's husband who had that very day set off on a training course and wouldn't be back before the end of the week.

As she said goodbye to Robert Beth noted that the infant seemed unduly listless. She was wondering whether to comment when Cassie gave her an opening.

'Robert doesn't seem himself today. Poor mite was sick earlier on. He doesn't seem to be able to keep anything down. If he doesn't buck up tomorrow I'll take him to the doctor. It's not like him to be off colour.'

Beth let her fingers rest on the baby's forehead. He felt OK. 'I'm sure it's nothing,' she said, but couldn't suppress a twinge of anxiety, although she told herself that there was no reason for it.

Once home she put Robert out of her mind but couldn't dismiss Dominic. She phoned Morven and got the same advice. 'Talk it over with Dominic.'

The reflection the mirror gave back to Beth was everything she could have wished. The dark green suit had remained one of her favourites and she felt the familiar surge of confidence she got when wearing it. Her hair and make-up were impeccable as always, but today she had taken just that little bit more care. She dropped the dark blue case of the Christian Dior lipstick into her handbag. If she stood here fiddling with her appearance any longer she'd start to get cold feet.

At some time, she realised, she had made a decision without ever consciously knowing she had done so.

There was no reason why she couldn't talk to Dominic in very general terms about her future and that she was thinking of leaving. From then on it would be up to him. Whatever happened, even if she discovered that he wanted her to go and even if he guessed that it was her feelings for him that were driving her into the move, she would feel better for having told him. Cassie was right. The worst thing would be to be left with a vague, nebulous regret, a feeling of if only, of what-might-have-been.

Whether her new resolve had communicated itself to Dominic or whether he had come to some decisions of his own, Beth didn't really know or care. All that mattered was that the tension between them seemed to have eased and he was smiling at her.

'Have dinner with me tonight, Bethesda.' Dominic might sound confident but one quick glance told Beth that he wasn't quite as sure of himself as he sounded. That in itself was enough to boost her confidence.

'Thank you.' She tried to remain composed as she smiled a reply, but when Dominic stretched out a hand to run a finger caressingly down her cheek she could feel her smile getting wider and wider. And that annoyed her. Why should I make it so easy for him? she fumed when, with a lazy smile, Dominic sauntered towards his office, telling her over his shoulder, 'I've been thinking and now we've got a lot of talking to do!'

'Too true,' she muttered inelegantly to herself.

It was the very unexpectedness of disasters which made them so shocking. One minute Beth's world was relatively calm and controlled and the next she could hardly take in what was happening.

By chance Dominic was in her office when the phone rang, just as he had been countless times before. Beth reached out and lifted the receiver and the world turned black. It took a moment before she could make any sense of the incoherent babbling coming through the receiver, and when she did her blood ran cold.

'Calm down and tell me exactly what's happened,' she instructed sharply, trying to stem the flow of Cassie's agitated outpourings and instil some calm into her friend. Out of the corner of her eye she saw Dominic's head come up from the papers he was scanning and his eyes focus on her as he took in her words and the tone of her voice. He didn't need to see the colour drain from her face to know that something was very wrong.

'Robert? Something's happened to Robert?' The words were torn from Beth and she felt as though her heart were being ripped from her. She listened for a second then cried, 'Oh, my God. Is he going to be all right? Where are you? What are they doing?' She was gabbling questions out, not giving Cassie time to reply, and feeling the hysteria rising in her when she felt a firm hand clasp her shoulder and she looked up, her eyes brimming with tears, to find a grim-faced Dominic watching her intently.

The pressure from his hand on her shoulder increased as their eyes met, almost as though he was trying to give her some of his strength. Taking heart from it, Beth briefly turned her head so that she could rub her cheek on the back of his hand as she swallowed and took a deep breath, before saying more calmly, 'Tell me where you are and I'll be on my way.' Seconds later she put down the phone and turned to Dominic.

'I have. . .'

'I know,' he interrupted her. 'I'll drive you. You're in no state to go anywhere on your own.' With that, he was reaching for her bag and coat and hustling her out of the office.

'What about. . .?' she began to ask.

He cut her off with an abrupt, 'It can all wait.'

Her nerveless fingers fumbled with the seat belt and when Dominic gently pried her hands from it and fastened her into her seat like a child she felt the tears she had been ruthlessly suppressing spill over and trickle down her cheeks. Giving a convulsive sob, she tried to check them. Dominic's hand came over hers to clasp it warmly, and his thumb rubbed comfortingly over her wrist as he soothed her.

'Don't cry, Beth, you're going to have to be brave for a while yet. Arriving at the hospital in floods of tears won't help you. Or Robert.'

'Poor Robert,' Beth wailed, her voice rising on a note of panic, but the pressure from Dominic's hands calmed her enough so that she could stifle her fears for the

moment and look at him with warm gratitude. 'Thank
you, Dominic.'

He merely grunted and turned on the ignition. 'Do
you know what's happened?' he asked, and Beth shook
her head.

'Not really. He hasn't been well for a couple of days.'
Her voice wobbled ominously and she fought for control.
'He *has* to be all right,' she declared vehemently. 'I love
him so much. I couldn't bear it if anything happened
to him.'

Fortunately they were still in the car park because the
car swerved violently to one side at her impassioned
words, causing Dominic to swear under his breath as
they narrowly missed scraping a parked Rover. Beth,
however, appeared not to notice the swerve or the tightening of Dominic's lips as he fought both for control of
the car and his next words.

'I didn't realise. . .' he muttered, almost to himself,
glancing at Beth who sat hunched in her seat, enveloped
in misery and sniffing bravely in an effort to stop the
tears from falling.

Steeling himself, Dominic reached out to pat Beth's
clasped hands once more. 'That's a good girl. We'll be
at the hospital soon.'

She nodded, staring straight ahead. 'Thank you.'

As he eased the car into the busy flow of traffic
Dominic realised that he didn't know which of the city's
busy hospitals they were going to. 'Where are we going,
Beth?' he asked as gently as he knew how.

'The hospital,' she told him, turning to look at him
with the expression of a bewildered child. Hadn't she
been saying that all along? Robert was in hospital.

'Yes,' Dominic said, still trying to sound soothing,
'but which one?'

For a second Beth looked at him blankly, as though
she didn't comprehend his meaning. Where else would

Robert be but at the Royal Hospital for Sick Children at Yorkhill?

'Yorkhill,' she answered, staring at Dominic as though there was something wrong with him.

Again the car swerved, earning Dominic a furious blast on the horn from the driver in the next lane and much shaking of fists.

'Yorkhill,' he muttered, his voice sounding strangled somewhere in the back of his throat. 'The Sick Kids?'

'Yes, yes. Where else would he be?' Beth demanded querulously, totally forgetting that she had led Dominic to believe that Robert was a grown man. Furthermore, a grown man with whom she was involved in a serious relationship.

Another glance at Beth's taut face convinced Dominic that now probably wasn't the best time to demand an explanation, but it was with a considerably lighter heart, and expression, that he set off for the children's hospital.

'Who phoned you?' he enquired, thinking that was a reasonably safe question, and one which might help him to understand a little of what was going on.

'Cassie,' Beth told him promptly, then rushed into agitated speech. 'You see, George is away all week on a training course...and she was all on her own...and... and I am his godmother,' she finished defiantly, as though daring Dominic to challenge her right to be dashing to the hospital. 'I had to go.'

'Of course you do, love,' he soothed, controlling his facial muscles rigidly, although he very much wanted to break out in a broad grin. Much as he was sorry for the child, a number of very loose ends were beginning to fall into place, trying themselves into nice, neat bows.

Beth was vaguely aware of Dominic organising them at the hospital. One look at Cassie, and the two friends had fallen into each other's arms amid floods of tears.

'They haven't told me anything,' Cassie wailed, looking at Beth and Dominic with wild, frightened eyes. 'What's happening to my baby?' she sobbed.

'I'll try to find out,' Dominic promised, 'but first tell us what happened.'

'He's been sick a few times over the last couple of days and crying, and. . .and. . .today he was so hot and sick all the time. Couldn't keep anything down at all. I called the GP and he came and arranged for us to come straight here.'

'Where's Robert now?' Beth asked, trying to make sense of the story.

'In X-Ray,' Cassie wailed.

'Mrs Simpson?' A young nurse was coming towards them. 'Would you like to come back and stay with Robert while we wait for the results of his X-ray?'

As she rushed after the nurse Cassie turned back to Beth. 'Come with me.'

Beth needed no second asking.

A few minutes later Dominic joined them, clutching two beakers of coffee. 'They're checking the films now and a doctor will come and talk to you soon,' he told Cassie, who was clutching at his arm. 'Is your husband on his way?' he asked, which caused a fresh flood of tears.

'I tried to phone George, but the number was engaged. It keeps being engaged. That was the final straw and I phoned you,' Cassie sobbed, now clutching Beth's hand so that both cups of coffee threatened to spill. Dominic relieved them of the coffee and tried to calm them both.

'Give me the number, Cassie, and I'll keep on until I get him,' he instructed, and then left the two women standing by the baby while Beth tried to calm and reassure her friend.

He returned to find a cheery young paediatric registrar with them and an X-ray on the lighted view-screen. 'As you can see,' the young man was saying, 'there looks to be a shadow, but it isn't very clear.'

'And you're sure?' Beth was demanding.

'Sure as I can be,' the young man replied, resolutely chirpy.

Beth thought he could do with a bit more *gravitas*, although she recognised that he had the right to feel pleased at making what could be a tricky diagnosis.

'What's it called again?' Cassie asked, clearly not following everything the registrar had just flung at her.

'Hypertrophic pyloric stenosis,' Dr Fraser told her with a grin. 'It doesn't show up clearly on the X-ray but you can feel it. There's a small lump, like a marble, in the epigastrium. It's sometimes referred to as pyloric tumour but, of course—'

Cassie cut him off. 'Tumour. My baby has a tumour!' She sagged at the word as the doctor carried on, unperturbed.

'—it isn't a tumour at all.'

'It's all right, Cassie,' Beth interjected. 'It's just a swelling.'

'Like a doughnut,' Dominic added, feeling that the time had come to make his presence felt.

'Indeed.' The young doctor picked up on the explanation again, glaring at both Beth and Dominic. 'There's a swelling like a doughnut around the stomach and duodenum which causes an obstruction and doesn't allow food to go from the stomach to the duodenum. That's why he's sick all the time. And he had a temperature because he's dehydrated.'

'And what are you going to do?'

'He's on a drip now to rehydrate him,' young Dr Fraser said, 'because all that vomiting has caused him to become dehydrated. Then we'll whisk him off to Theatre for a quick operation. I'll need to get you to fill in the consent forms.'

'Operation.' Cassie's voice was now no more than a strangled squawk.

'It's nothing much—' Dr Fraser began, but was interrupted by both Beth and Dominic.

'It doesn't take long—'

'It'll be over quickly—'

'Yes,' cut in Dr Fraser, 'it's a simple process. We cut
the swelling to remove the obstruction. When he comes
round he'll start drinking straight away and be fine in no
time at all.'

'Are you sure?' Cassie demanded.

'Positive,' all three doctors responded in chorus.

Cassie crumpled again as Robert was wheeled away
to Theatre, and Dominic took that moment to divert her
attention by informing her that he had got through to
George, who would be with her in less than two hours.
He then settled the two women in a quiet corner out of
the way of prying eyes, and sat down to await George's
arrival. Then he would be able to take Beth home and
ask some questions himself.

CHAPTER TEN

WAS this, Beth contemplated, what was known as 'the moment of truth'? George had arrived at the hospital and was comforting his wife; Robert was out of Theatre, drinking and well on the way to a full recovery; she had given way and had a good cry and consequently was feeling much better for the release of her pent-up feelings, and Dominic—at this very moment Dominic was in her kitchen, making them coffee.

From the moment of Cassie's phone call she had to admit that he had behaved impeccably. No, if she was honest, it was more than that. He had behaved like a real friend. There had been no question but that he would take her to the hospital or that he would stay with her, offering her whatever support he could. And all that had been offered before he realised that Robert wasn't her boyfriend but her very young godson.

With startling clarity, Beth remembered how the car had swerved when she had told him to drive to Yorkhill—the children's hospital. He had not demanded an explanation of her then, but he would now. How was she to confess to him that she had lied to him? It hadn't been deliberate, she justified herself, rather that she hadn't corrected his mistaken interpretation of a few overheard phone calls. Lying by omission, Dominic would no doubt point out, was still lying. Would he wonder if she had lied elsewhere?

As the door was pushed open by a beautifully shod foot Beth wondered if she could squeeze out a few more tears. The thought crossed her mind that if she could keep crying, Dominic wouldn't push her to answer any awkward questions. He might even hold her again and let her cry comfortably into his shirt front. Hanging her head, she tried a few experimental sniffs and snivels. It would be nice to be held and comforted again, as he had held her while she'd cried in the car on leaving the hospital. He had been so patient with her then.

A quick peep from under her lashes showed a damp patch of darker blue on his otherwise pristine person. Her tears. The intimate picture it conjured up made her quickly lower her eyes again. Dominic would want answers and she didn't have the faintest idea of what she was going to say to him.

The mug came into her line of vision, gripped in a strong, male hand, and was carefully lowered onto the coffee-table. The hand hovered for a second, then withdrew. Still she didn't look up.

'Feeling better, Bethesda?' Dominic enquired conversationally. 'A good cry always releases tension.'

How would he know that? Beth asked herself cynically. When did he last have a good cry? Despite his words, the tone of his voice told her that he was running out of patience playing the kind, supportive friend who was content to let her deal with her feelings in her own way. He sounded as though he was about to demand some answers.

Covertly watching him out of the corner of one eye, she observed him take up position in one of her armchairs—his mug of coffee within easy reach. The outward appearance of a relaxed man at one with the world was, Beth sensed, a cover for inner tension which kept the slight smile that curved his lips from reaching his eyes. When she could bear the silence no longer she reached for her coffee, and that simple action relaxed whatever restraint Dominic had put on himself.

'Well, Bethesda?'

She knew full well that he wanted an explanation of

her entire behaviour over Robert, not just today's upset, but since she still didn't know where, or how, to begin she took refuge in prudent silence. And a pathetic sniff. It didn't work.

'Godson, Bethesda?' His voice sounded faintly ironic and that touched Beth on a raw nerve.

'Is it so odd that I should have a godson?' she asked with an attempt at haughty disdain which didn't, alas, ring true.

'Not at all.' Dominic sounded blandly indifferent. 'But it does seem odd that you should try to pass him off as your lover.'

'I didn't. Not intentionally. It was your mistake,' she told him futilely, knowing that Dominic wasn't going to let go.

'You could easily have pointed out my error,' he replied with irrefutable logic. 'What interests me is *why* you didn't. Why you apparently *wanted* me to believe he was your lover.'

'Don't keep saying that!' It sounded to Beth that Dominic was taking particular delight in lingering over the word 'lover', imbuing it with sensual overtones which were having the most unsettling effect on her pulse rate.

'Why not?' he enquired smoothly. 'Does it make you feel uncomfortable now that you've been found out?'

Yes, Beth wanted to say, but couldn't bring herself to be that honest. Despite a quickly gulped mouthful of too-hot coffee, Beth's mouth felt dry and she struggled to get the words out. Dominic's patience was wearing thin, however, and it was only when he exploded into vehement speech that Beth understood just how angry he was under the controlled façade.

'And so you damn well should be! Do you realise what I've been thinking all these weeks?'

'Dominic, I—'

'I've never thought of you as a liar before.'

'I'm not,' she declared hotly, stung to retaliation, but the scathing glance he gave her, leaning forward as though to leap out of the chair at her, was enough to render her silent.

'What do you call all the fairy stories you've been spinning me—about Robert having to work late and miss dinner, to name but one? That wasn't simply not putting me right, that was out-and-out deliberate lying!'

Fiery red rushed to Beth's cheeks and she turned her head away, incapable of looking him in the face and lying. Or facing him and telling the truth, come to that. She *had* lied to him about Robert—there was no getting around that.

'I'm waiting, Bethesda.' And by the sound of it not for much longer.

Taking what remained of her courage in both hands, Beth turned to face him. 'It seemed a good idea at the time.'

The narrowing of Dominic's eyes told her that he didn't appreciate the levity, and she hurried to make good her statement. 'Sorry if that sounds flippant, but at the time I didn't stop to think. When you assumed that Robert was a man. . .I was going to explain, but somehow I got sidetracked. Afterwards it didn't seem important. Then, later, when you did it again. . .' She shrugged. 'I don't know. . .I can't explain. . . It just seemed—'

'I know. "A good idea at the time."' Some of the anger drained away and Dominic fell back in the comfortable embrace of the armchair. Not that that made Beth feel any easier. It was still like being caught in the hypnotic stare of a predatory animal.

'There's more to this than you're telling me,' Dominic observed smoothly, 'but I don't think now is the time to demand any more answers.' He grinned at the audible sigh of relief which escaped from Beth. 'But I expect you to remember my. . .generosity and kindness to you now, Bethesda, when I *do* demand some answers. You're in a highly emotional state, and I don't want to be accused of taking unfair advantage of you. So, against my better judgement, I'm going now, leaving you to recover on your own. If you need me you can call me at the office.'

Beth could hardly believe the reprieve she had been granted, and felt she ought to make some attempt at regaining her normal composure. 'If you'd just give me a couple of minutes I'll come back with you.' Her hands flew to her face as the realisation of what her tears must have done to her face, to her make-up, hit her. She must look a total fright, which Dominic confirmed without her needing to say a word.

'It would take more than a couple of minutes to repair the damage, Bethesda. You look remarkably like a red-nosed panda at the moment. A blushing, red-nosed panda,' he added teasingly, as embarrassment made her cheeks flood with colour. As she would have turned away from him he caught her wrist and pulled her back to him, his hand lifting and tilting her chin to look directly into her face.

'On you, tears and smudged mascara look good,' he told her gently, and apparently honestly, and threw her into total bewilderment as he dropped a light kiss on the tip of her still-red nose.

'There's not much of the day left. There's no need to come in and you still have to get over the shock,' he said, the look in his eyes causing Beth's knees to buckle alarmingly, only to alter the mood as he added, 'We can't have you coming in looking like this—you'll frighten the entire workforce and everything will grind to a halt as I explain that I have not resorted to beating you. Not that you don't deserve it.'

The last was added so evenly—almost as an after-thought—that it took Beth several seconds before its meaning sank in. And several more before she could

think of a retort. By then it was too late and she heard
the sound of the front door closing after Dominic's
retreating figure.

It wasn't as though she was expecting anyone so why
was she so restless? Beth roamed around her flat, unable
to settle to anything. Robert was going to be all right so
it wasn't worry over him that was making her so edgy,
unable to sit and concentrate on anything. She pressed
the plunger down on her cafetière and wondered briefly
if too much caffeine was the trouble. Maybe she
shouldn't drink any more. The glass pot of the dark,
fragrant brew beckoned and she poured herself a cup.

The loud, insistent sound of the doorbell shattered the
silence, causing her to spill coffee on the counter top.
She didn't wait to wipe up the liquid but rushed into
the hall, dragging fingers through her dark curly hair—
frantically trying to fluff it up as she snatched a hurried
look in the pewter-framed mirror.

Now she could honestly face up to the source of her
restlessness. She had been waiting for Dominic to come
back, as she had known he would. Her heart plummeted
as she reached to open the door. Maybe she was wrong.
Maybe it would be a neighbour or Cassie, full of news
about Robert. Her heart was in her mouth as she swung
open the door and almost cried out with relief to see
Dominic standing there.

'Hello, Bethesda.' He kissed her lightly on the lips as
he moved past her, almost casually thrusting a bunch of
deep peach roses into her hands. 'Mmm. Coffee.' He
headed for the kitchen, leaving Beth—struck dumb—
inanely clutching the open door.

It took something of an effort to pull herself together
and push the door closed. Since late afternoon she had
been hoping that Dominic would come back, dreaming
about what it might mean if he did. And now he

was here, and she was too numb to react.

A sudden sharp pain brought her out of her trance and she glanced down at the hand which had inadvertently tightened its grip on the roses, only to contact a sharp thorn. A timely reminder, she thought. Dominic might bring her roses, but she still had to remember that he, too, came with thorns.

And if she wasn't going to let him walk all over her she had better start asserting herself immediately. He had no right to walk in and take over her flat.

He crossed the hall to the living room, a cup of coffee in each hand. Giving her a quick appraising glance, as though not at all surprised to see her still standing there like some lifesized doll, he said, 'Put those in water and come and join me. We've got a lot of talking to do.'

The words were becoming a refrain. Why was it they never actually finished their talks?

She very nearly disobeyed him. Who was he to be handing out orders in *her* flat? But the heady scent of the roses assailed her nostrils and she knew she couldn't sacrifice the flowers to bad temper.

Searching out the tall, cut-glass vase which had been her grandmother's, Beth took her time arranging the long-stemmed flowers. Not that they looked any different when she carried them into her living room ten minutes later than they had when she had first dropped them in the vase. The flowers spoke for themselves and needed hardly any arranging.

Was it a good sign or a bad sign that Dominic didn't comment on how long she had been? He was lounging back on the sofa, coffee in hand, looking too much at home for Beth's peace of mind. And too familiar. They had played this scene once too often.

'Come and join me.' As she would have seated herself in one of the armchairs, Dominic's hand darted out to close round her wrist, pulling her towards him. She tried to resist but he was stronger than she was and rather than risk an ungainly struggle—one she was almost certain to lose—she allowed herself to be pulled down onto the sofa next to him. Still keeping tight hold of her wrist, he leaned across and placed a kiss—if the light, feathery touching of his lips could be called that—just below her ear.

'Now that we don't have to think about Robert,' he murmured, the teasing touch of his lips tracing a path down her throat to nestle in the hollow at its base, 'it's time that we concentrated on us.'

'Us?' Beth's voice was no more than a squeak as she sat rigidly still, trying to pretend that this was not happening.

'Yes, us.' Dominic's voice was muffled as he began the journey back to her ear. His warm, moist breath caressed her skin, raising goose bumps, and she couldn't suppress a shiver.

'Cold, Betheseda?' he enquired solicitously, a wicked glint darkening his eyes to almost black. They both knew that cold had nothing to do with it, and excitement everything.

'Dominic.'

'Mmm.'

'Dominic.' This time her voice sounded steadier, more in control, but Dominic responded to that by pulling on her wrist and taking her with him as he fell back into the corner of the sofa with Beth draped across him. He let go of her wrist to wrap both arms around her, his breath fanning her cheek. Her heartbeat escalating rapidly, Beth found that she had nothing to say. Nothing sensible, that was.

'What were you going to say?' His voice was deep, husky, relaxed, and just feeling his chest move as he spoke caused Beth to shiver again.

'Mmm.' It was her turn to mumble as she snuggled

against him, feeling his arm tighten around her—even as she wondered what on earth she was doing.

'You seemed to be trying to get my attention.' One of Dominic's hands threaded itself through her hair and pulled her head back gently so that he could look down into her face. There was a lazy smile about his lips and laughter lines fanning out from the corners of his eyes.

He held her gaze, his smile deepening, but there was something...something indefinable that Beth couldn't quite put her finger on and which made her wary. Suddenly she didn't trust Dominic at all, and that made lying in his arms very uncomfortable. Pushing herself away from him, she struggled to sit up and was somewhat surprised when Dominic let her go with no show of resistance.

'You said you wanted to talk,' she reminded him.

'I've changed my mind.' Was there an edge to the slow drawl? He didn't say enough for Beth to decide.

'Why?' Dumb question, Beth, she told herself. The reason was perfectly obvious. Dominic must have thought the same as his lips curved in a truly wicked grin as he reached for her again.

'I'd rather make love to you,' he told her with no hesitation and no embarrassment.

But good sense and innate shyness were overtaking Beth. She didn't feel comfortable with Dominic, although she was honest enough to admit—at least to herself— that she wanted to make love with him as much as he obviously wanted her.

'But. . .'

'But what?' His voice, indistinct again as his mouth resumed its tantalising kisses, didn't seem to be speaking so much as breathing the words.

'You said. . .' Beth's voice was coming in gasps as his lips caressed her jaw line, hovered near her mouth, but never claimed it. '. . .you wanted to talk. . .' The sentence was lost as a moan of pleasure escaped her. '. . .about us,' she finished valiantly.

'Us.' Dominic stilled for a moment, his lips thinning suddenly into a tight, hard line and his face taking on deep, harsh lines as the dim lighting threw strange shadows across it. 'Now there's no Robert I have to worry about,' he was telling her easily, 'I think there is—there can be—us.'

When she didn't say anything the hand still buried in her hair turned her head towards him. 'Can't there?'

He seemed to be looking for some kind of confirmation, and for a second Beth saw the tautness in his face not as harshness but as uncertainty, vulnerability. Her loving heart went out to him and she pushed aside all her own uncertainties and leaned forward into his embrace.

'Yes. There is us.'

His eyes darkened with desire and an expression flashed through them which Beth could not decipher. It wasn't happiness, but why should she think it was pain? Then his mouth was finally, gloriously, on hers and she stopped wondering—stopped thinking about anything except the feel, the taste of Dominic as his tongue pushed past her teeth to invade the intimacy of her mouth. Time itself seemed to stop as she gave herself up to the magic of his touch.

She had no idea when, or how, she had lost her blouse and then her bra, or when Dominic had discarded his shirt. It was only as the soft wiriness of the hairs on his chest rubbed against the tender flesh of her breasts that she realised they were both half-naked, and that if Dominic had anything to do with it they would both soon be fully naked.

Her body tensed, even as her hands sought out the firm muscles of his chest, the hard flatness of his stomach. She did and she didn't want to make love with him. Making

love with Dominic would be wonderful, but. . . With a
blinding flash she remembered Marianne. How could she
possibly have forgotten the other woman? Shame that
she had forgotten threatened to overwhelm her, and her
body tensed.

When he had first arrived she would have sworn that
he was excited as she had been, that he had been waiting
to get back to her to sort out the muddle they had got
into. To put straight things between them once and for
all. But he hadn't mentioned the other girl. And that was
creating a barrier between them. That he still wanted
Beth wasn't in dispute. What was were his feelings for
her. She still couldn't believe that he cared, not in the
way she wanted him to care. The way she cared.

Her tenseness communicated itself to Dominic, who
muttered in her ear, 'Relax, sweetheart, I'm not going to
hurt you.' His fingers ran down her spine, causing her
whole body to tremble while her mind rejected his words.
Somehow they sounded cold, calculated, impersonal.

She tried to push away from him but found her legs
trapped, entwined with his. Eventually he let her go and
as she sat up he caught her upper arms, twisting her to
face him when she would have turned away. Embarrassed
by her nakedness, Beth couldn't meet his eyes, but
Dominic appeared totally oblivious to her unease.

'Tell me, Bethesda,' he demanded, shaking her gently,
then more forcefully when she reminded silent, 'what's
the matter? Tell me.'

'Nothing, except this is a mistake. I'm upset and emotional because of Robert.' She used the excuse to salvage
some pride. 'I'm sorry if I misled you. I never intended
to. I'm fond of you, Dominic—'

'Fond,' Dominic snarled. 'Fond!' His grip tightened.
'I don't believe you.' His voice lost its strident tone and
when he added, 'Please,' Beth almost gave in. He had
sounded close to pleading with her.

Dumbly she shook her head, then forced herself to look at him. 'I don't know what you mean,' she told him steadily, while part of her was dying inside at the denial of her love. 'I'm sorry.'

Her resignation was written and waiting to be handed to Dominic. It had been written the moment Dominic had left. There was to be no more dithering. Managing to avoid him all day and knowing that it was a cowardly thing to do, she left it on his desk at the end of the day. She would face him tomorrow. She would have to work her notice out but this was the end. Tears welled into her eyes as she left his room and blinded by them, she didn't see the woman until she had almost bumped into her and heard a voice enquiring solicitously, 'Beth, what's happened? What's the matter?'

Marianne.

'Nothing,' Beth choked out, barely able to speak through the lump of tears in her throat.

'Yes, there is. Is it something to do with your godson?'

So she knew about that! What else had Dominic told her? Beth shook her head, beyond words.

'Then what's that stupid brother of mine done now?'

The impact of the words halted Beth in her headlong flight, and even put a brake on the flow of tears. 'Your brother?' she gasped, forcing the words out.

'Dominic,' Marianne responded impatiently. 'What did he do to upset you? I told him last night. . .' She stopped, struck by Beth's expression. 'You did *know* he was my brother, didn't you?' she asked more softly.

But Beth couldn't reply. Shaking free of the loose grip Marianne had on her arm, she ran from the building.

There was never a taxi when you wanted one. Beth had sat in her car for five minutes swallowing her sobs, before accepting that she was in no fit state to drive. It had

taken her another five minutes to find a taxi through the
blur of tears. Having arrived at her flat, as she groped in
her bag for money to pay the driver the door was opened
and she was practically hauled onto the pavement.
Dominic paid the driver without letting go of his hold
on her. A Dominic who looked tense and not a little
grim, but in whom anger had been replaced by a new
kind of energy. An energy that could be excitement.

As she stumbled over the kerb Dominic took a firmer
hold on her arm, almost as though he expected her to
run away again, but Beth had no more energy for that.
Numbly she allowed herself to be led into the building
and helped upstairs to her flat. She daren't think what
Dominic's presence might mean. To begin to hope again,
only to be dashed down, would be more than she could
bear. It would be the end of her. Instinctively she moved
towards the living room but Dominic held her back.

'No. Not in there. That room has a jinx on it,' Dominic
declared. 'Every time I try to talk to you in there something goes wrong.'

'Where, then?' Beth cast a covert glance towards her
bedroom door. He surely couldn't mean. . .

'In here.' Before her wayward thoughts could fully
form Dominic was ushering her into the kitchen and
pushing her into one of the straight-backed chairs at the
table. Miraculously her tears had dried and she was feeling more optimistic by the minute.

'The ritual coffee, I think,' Dominic was saying as he
filled the kettle and plugged it in, 'and then a proper,
serious talk, with no holding back.'

'*Do* we have anything to talk about?' Beth asked, her
emotions in an uproar.

Dominic ran an unsteady hand through his hair, the
resulting untidiness making him look even more dear to
Beth. 'Nothing has been straightforward since I came
back from the States and found that my Beth had

disappeared and a stranger was in her place.'

'Stranger?' This wasn't what Beth expected to hear and she gazed at him in consternation. Maybe Cassie and Morven had been right in suggesting that her change would have more of an impact on Dominic than she had given credence. Dominic looked thoroughly confused, too, and he turned back to the safety of making the coffee and putting the mugs on the table before taking a seat opposite her.

'You told me—' she started to say, but Dominic interrupted her.

'I know, I know. It's all my fault. But I was so shocked when I walked in and found this. . .transformation. All I had been thinking about while I was away was how much I was missing you. It took me two weeks before I could admit to myself that that was what the problem was. Then I couldn't wait to get back to see you. I had such plans.'

'I don't believe you.' Beth stated the words calmly and without due emphasis and sat back, waiting to hear what Dominic would say next. None of this rang true.

He had the grace to look slightly shamefaced. 'It's true all right, even if I was struggling to accept it, and it's much clearer in hindsight. You have to understand, Beth, that realising how far you had got under my skin came as something of a shock. I wasn't planning on settling down, but I knew you wouldn't agree to a brief affair. And then I had to admit to myself that that wasn't what I wanted either. But commitment. . .I didn't think I was ready for that.'

'You were shocked you could feel anything for some-body like me. . .someone who looked like I did?' she asked, seeking clarification from him, and was amazed to see how angry he suddenly looked.

'Don't put yourself down,' he instructed sharply. 'The new Bethesda might look more sophisticated and be etter dressed, but the old Beth had a grace, a tranquility, hat shone out of her restrained style and that was—is— ar superior to all the new make-up.'

'You don't like—?' she queried, unable to formulate he question clearly.

'You're beautiful now, Bethesda,' he told her, 'but ou were beautiful before. I know you can't go back to eing how you were before, and I wouldn't want you to ose all the positive things you've gained. It's wonderful o see your increase in confidence, but it is important to ne that you don't think you *have* to look like this.'

'But I thought. . .I tried—'

'I know.' His hand stole across the table top to take old of hers, squeezing it tightly when she tried to draw way. 'Beth, I think I must have been in love with you or years, but I didn't know it. It was hearing you call ne names that started bringing me to my senses, not this ransformation. I knew it for certain when Helena ttacked you. If you did it for me. . . *Did* you do it for ne?' he asked abruptly, as though suddenly realising that erhaps he had presumed too much.

This time it was Beth who held onto his hand when ne would have let go.

'Partly,' she conceded honestly. 'But partly for me, oo. You walked all over me, Dominic,' she told him, miling slightly to take some of the sting from the words, and I let you. I don't know why, or how it happened, ut one day I just knew that I. . .we. . .couldn't go on ike that. You were right. I had to learn to stand up for nyself.'

'But you were gentle—'

'And tranquil, and calm, and all the other things,' she nterrupted him. 'I know. But doesn't it all sound a bit. . . vet? I was a wimp!'

'Not at all,' he defended hotly. 'It was—'

'If you say feminine I'll kick you,' Beth told him

straight faced, suddenly secure in herself and the future.
The light in Dominic's eyes informed her that the outcome of this conversation could only go one way, no
matter how they got there.

'There's strength as well as weakness in those quali-
ties, Beth,' he reminded her seriously. 'Don't throw away
the best parts.'

'I'll do my best,' she replied, removing her hand from
his and leaning back in the hard chair—causing his eyebrows to climb up his forehead alarmingly.

Then he grinned again. 'Good!' Quickly he became
serious once more. 'I'd just read your letter and thought
everything was over—that I'd lost you for ever—when
Marianne burst in. *My sister*, Marianne.' He came to
kneel by her, wrapping his arms around her and drawing
her close. For a second she tried to hold herself still
before she succumbed to the need to nestle against him,
her face burrowed into his shoulder. She felt his breath
fan her cheek as he murmured, 'Bethesda, how could
you be so *stupid*? She's my sister.'

'I didn't know that.' Beth tried to defend herself.

'No wonder you were always pushing me away,' he
mused. 'Why didn't you say anything? Ask me?'

'I didn't want to hear that you cared for her. That I
was second best.'

'Never that. You could never be that.' He kissed her
again, a trail of light kisses along her jaw which were
proving very distracting. 'You must have thought I was
being very deceitful.'

'Um, yes.'

His mouth returned to hers and the kiss deepened as
his tongue again parted her teeth to enter the warm cavern
of her mouth. Beth groaned and melted against him.

'But no more so than I thought you were being over
Robert.'

That brought her up with a jolt and she struggled in

his embrace, but now that he had her Dominic wasn't going to let go. His lips claimed hers and as his hands moved across her body, moulding her to him, Beth felt any remaining doubt and uncertainty vanish as Dominic whispered, 'I love you so much, Bethesda, my own Beth.'

Now it was safe to say, 'I love you, too, Dominic. For so long. I didn't know it either.'

It was several minutes before either of them spoke again. 'You will marry me, won't you?' He kissed her. 'You never did give me a good reason why not. Your last objection doesn't hold any more. Not now you love me. You don't know what it did to me when you told me my love wasn't enough.'

'I never did.' Beth sounded positively scandalised.

'You most certainly did.' His arms tightened around her as he remembered the pain.

'When? How. . .?' Had he taken leave of his senses? If he had told her he loved her she would have taken notice!

'When I first asked you to marry me. You said we didn't love each other and I knew then that nothing else would matter in life if you didn't love me—wouldn't marry me.'

'But you didn't say anything. . .'

'You were adamant that you didn't want to marry me. I asked if one person loving was enough and you said no.' His voice sounded so bleak with remembered pain that Beth turned in his arms to press her lips against his, this time her tongue demanding entry to his mouth. As she was sinking into the sensual pleasure he was arousing in her she faintly remembered she still had something to say.

'No,' she mumbled against his lips.

'Yes,' he breathed, arching her body to his.

'No. I mean not no to this. . .no to. . .' but her words were punctuated by kisses and she knew she was losing any sense of control. She had to explain to Dominic before that happened. Gently she pushed him away.

'Let me explain,' she begged when Dominic tried to retain his hold on her.

'Explain what?' he muttered against her mouth, his tongue teasing its corners and causing tremors throughout her body.

'I wasn't rejecting you—saying your love wasn't enough,' she explained. 'I didn't understand what you meant,' she told him honestly.

'What did you think I meant, then?' Dominic sounded confused and Beth could hardly blame him. Little in their relationship had been straightforward. 'You certainly sounded as though you knew what you were talking about.'

'I thought you meant me. I thought you had realised that I loved you. And I knew, no matter how much I loved you, that—'

'You loved me then?' Dominic's amazement was complete. 'But I thought... You never indicated... Sometimes I. . .' He trailed off in disbelief. 'When I think of all the time we've wasted!'

'If only I'd understood. But all I could think of was that in the end being married to you and knowing you didn't love me would be worse than not being with you.'

'And that's why you turned me down?'

She nodded. 'That's why I turned you down. Because I thought it was some kind of weird gesture on your part to—'

He cut her off. 'I don't think I want to know any more. You seem to have been determined to think badly of me. And that has to stop—now!'

'Mmm.' Beth was only too happy to agree as she took her turn to trail kisses along his jaw, to end up nibbling gently on his ear lobe.

'You still haven't answered me,' he pointed out some minutes later, although from the expression on his face

Beth knew that he could be in no doubt about her answer.

She thought about her assertiveness classes and all the effort she had put into learning to say no, and meaning it when she said it. But also learning that it wasn't always necessary or appropriate to say no. Sometimes saying yes took courage too. As she contemplated a future without Dominic she knew with no question of doubt that courage had nothing to do with it. There was only one sensible answer she could give.

'Yes, Dominic.'

He swept her up into his arms. 'I think the kitchen has served its purpose in breaking the jinx,' he announced in a self-satisfied tone. 'Now I think we should go somewhere more comfortable so that I can make love to you. Properly. At last.'

He headed towards the bedroom, then stopped. 'You haven't said anything.' He started to sound worried. 'Have I done something wrong? Have you any objections?'

Beth grinned delightedly. It *had* been worth it. If ever there was a time to say no and mean it, it was now. She brushed her lips across his and took a reassuring breath.

'No, Dominic.'

MILLS & BOON®

Medical Romance™

Dear Santa,

Please make this a special Christmas for us.
This Christmas we would like...

A VERY SPECIAL NEED by Caroline Anderson
'Daddy do you think you'll ever find another mummy
for me? I think I'd like to have a mummy,' Alice asked.

A HEALING SEASON by Jessica Matthews
Libby's children loved having Dr Caldwell around at
Christmas, but then it wasn't just the children who
liked him.

MERRY CHRISTMAS, DOCTOR DEAR by Elisabeth Scott
Colin told his Uncle Matt that you couldn't always be
sure what you got for Christmas, you just had to wait
and see, but they felt sure that this Christmas would be
worth waiting for.

A FATHER FOR CHRISTMAS by Meredith Webber
Richard tries hard to put his feelings for Margaret's
children down to a lack of sleep, but he isn't fooling
anybody, not least of all himself!

*Christmas
is for kids*

...a family.
Thank you very much
The Children

Four books written by four authors from around
the world with one wish for Christmas.

GET TO KNOW
THE BEST OF ENEMIES

the latest blockbuster from TAYLOR SMITH

Who would you trust with your life? Think again.

*Linked to a terrorist bombing, a young student goes
missing. One woman believes in the girl's innocence
and is determined to find her before she is silenced.
Leya Nash has to decide—quickly—who to trust.
The wrong choice could be fatal.*

—

Valid only in the UK & Ireland against purchases made in retail outlets
and not in conjunction with any Reader Service or other offer.

50ᵖ OFF
COUPON
VALID UNTIL: 28.2.1998
TAYLOR SMITH'S *THE BEST OF ENEMIES*

To the Customer: This coupon can be used in part payment for a
copy of Taylor Smith's THE BEST OF ENEMIES. Only one coupon can
be used against each copy purchased. Valid only in the UK & Ireland
against purchases made in retail outlets and not in conjunction with
any Reader Service or other offer. Please do not attempt to redeem
this coupon against any other product as refusal to accept may cause
embarrassment and delay at the checkout.

To the Retailer: Harlequin Mills & Boon will redeem this coupon at
face value provided only that it has been taken in part payment for a
copy of Taylor Smith's THE BEST OF ENEMIES. The company reserves
the right to refuse payment against misredeemed coupons. Please
submit coupons to: Harlequin Mills & Boon Ltd. NCH Dept 730,
Corby, Northants NN17 INN.

9 904170 200509 >

0472 00189